BROKEN SURRENDER

SURRENDER SERIES 4

LORI KING

One bullet made it physically impossible for Sarah Bryant to fulfill her dreams of a military career. With her family's sympathy suffocating her, she escapes to Stone River, Texas, determined to rebuild a life and maybe find a new dream.

Silas and Jeremy are two brothers who are as different as Texas is big. One is an adrenaline-fueled former Army medic, the other a laid back tow truck business owner. The two things they have in common? They know they want to live life in a ménage relationship, and Sarah is the woman for them.

Sarah has too many doubts about herself to believe she can be enough for one man let alone two. Can these souls find what they need to grow together, or will they leave more emotional scars to match their physical ones?

This Veteran's Day, find home in the heart of our heroes with Broken Surrender, part of the Red Hot Heroes multi-author series and stands alone for reading enjoyment.

For the warriors who returned home missing pieces of themselves.
Thank you.

CHAPTER ONE

THE MELODIC SOUND of Blake Shelton's newest country hit, "Lonely Tonight," echoed out the lowered window, and drifted on the soft summer breeze. It was muggy in South Texas, and storms were predicted for later in the afternoon, but at the moment, the sky was a clear blue without a cloud in sight. From where Silas White was parked, he could see the crossing guard helping school children cross the one main road through Stone River. Beside him, his partner, Colby Bruce, snored loudly in his seat. It was a normal day, and he was bored out of his mind.

Just once he'd like to have some excitement. It was part of why he'd become a paramedic—that, and there wasn't much else for a veteran Army medic to do in this part of Texas without more education. When he came back from overseas, he'd had no interest in returning to school just to receive a degree he didn't really want. All he wanted was to help people and feel necessary in a world that suddenly didn't need him anymore. He missed the adrenaline rush of being on the front lines, but he damn sure didn't miss getting shot at. Hell, in some cases, being the medic was the most dangerous job in the military. He was the one who had to rush to the aid of the injured while bullets whizzed past his ears.

A bee chose that moment to land on the top of his ear, and he knocked it away with a curse. If only he could find something to rev him

1

up. A reason to wake up in the morning that didn't have him chugging back coffee like it was going out of style.

The radio on the dashboard of the ambulance crackled, and Silas surged to life as though he'd been electrocuted. He snatched up the handset before Colby could reach for it and spoke clearly into it. "Bus 14 to base, we're here. Over."

"Base to 14, call out to 104 Spitz Street. Just outside the apartment, there appears to be a woman injured. The manager wasn't sure what was wrong, but he said she was on the ground next to her car, and she wasn't moving. Over."

"Got it, Deanna. We're on our way." Turning the key in the ignition, Silas eased the large vehicle into the street just as Colby hit the switch for the lights and sirens.

Ahead of them, the school children pointed and waved as they zipped by, and Silas couldn't help but smile. At least someone was excited to see them. Most days, they just sat around doing nothing until the time clock dinged for them to go home, but sometimes, they got lucky and got to go and see the kids at the school. That was always fun.

"Wonder what we've got." Colby sat up a bit straighter and fixed his sagging badge on his shirt. "Heart attack? Stroke?"

"Heat exhaustion most likely," Silas said with a laugh.

"Wouldn't surprise me," Colby agreed. "Damned hot even for August."

They turned the corner, approaching the address from the east side, and the late afternoon sun blinded Silas for a moment, making him squint to see the apartment building they'd been called to. A low-slung building built back in the seventies, it was one of only three apartment complexes left in Stone River, and this was the cheapest of the bunch. A stranger might assume it was a former motel by the way the doors lined one side, each one with a perfectly matched window next to it and two parking stalls in front. These tiny apartments weren't meant to hold much, but they were always full.

A blue, two-door car that had obviously seen a lot of miles sat parked in front of the door on the end farthest from them, and a bald man stood near the back end of the car waving his arms around to get their attention.

"Hey Bob, what d'you got for us today?" Silas asked after parking the ambulance and jumping out. Colby followed with the med bag, and they both hurried to the female now seated on the ground with her back against the hot metal door of the car.

"She just fell over. Like something struck her, but now, she says she's fine." Bob Gunderson owned and managed the tiny apartment building. He was probably one of the nosiest people Silas knew, but at the moment, that might be a good thing.

"Ma'am, can you tell us what happened?" Colby asked.

Silas squatted down next to her, and reached for her, pushing her chin up with his fingers so that he could see her better. When she tipped her head back, he felt like he'd been sucker punched.

"Corporal Bryant?"

"Sergeant White?" Confusion filled her oversized green eyes. "What are you doing here?"

"At the moment, I'm rescuing a damsel in distress," he said playfully, earning a small smile as a reward.

"I'm not in distress. I'm fine. I just fell," she said, avoiding his curiosity by turning her head to watch what Colby was doing.

"That was an awfully strange fall, Miss Bryant," Bob argued. "Looked like you just locked up and then buckled from the middle."

"Did you hurt yourself when you fell, Sarah? Hit your head?" Silas asked, gripping her chin more firmly, this time to hold her head in place while he used his flashlight to check her pupils.

"No, not at all. I bruised my pride more than my ass. I promise you, I'm fine." She shook her head and brushed his hands away, her full lips firming into a tight pout.

Silas exchanged a look with Colby who shrugged his shoulders and proceeded to put away the supplies he'd just removed from the med bag. Something felt off about the way Sarah was responding, and he wasn't buying her no injuries claim. If she'd really just slipped and fallen, why didn't she get back up and brush herself off? Why sit in the hot sun against an equally hot car?

"All right. Well, I can't throw you over my shoulder and haul you to the hospital, but I can offer to help you up and back inside." Silas stood and held his hand out to her.

As expected, she stared at it in horror and shook her head. "I'm fine right here, thanks. You boys can go on about your business."

Planting his hands on his hips, he laughed. "So to avoid telling me what's really wrong, you're going to sit in the gravel with the sun burning you up to a crisp?"

She rolled her eyes and wrinkled her nose. "I'm telling you, I'm fine—"

"Prove it." He waited with his hands on his hips as she considered his challenge. There was fire in her eyes; the woman he knew from years ago could never resist a dare. For just a moment, he thought she was going to launch herself to her feet and punch him in the jaw for being an asshole, but then her eyes dropped and she shook her head sadly.

"I can't." Her words were soft, so he dropped back down beside her, conscious of the way she kept her gaze lowered and the responding twitch of his cock in his pants. Damn, he loved a feisty woman when she submitted.

"Tell me what's going on, Sarah."

He saw her grit her teeth and glance toward Colby and Bob before she hissed, "My back spasmed, and locked up. I just need to sit still for a bit until the muscle relaxer kicks in."

"Muscle relaxer? When did you take it?"

"A few minutes ago when Bob brought me a bottle of water. I swear I'll be fine."

He nodded in understanding. "Does this happen a lot? Random back spasms?"

"Too often for my taste," she admitted. Her phone beeped and she dug it out of her purse, wincing when she twisted her upper body.

"You know it's possible you hurt yourself when you fell and didn't realize it because of the spasm." He was determined to get her to at least let him check her over. Even if she refused to go to the hospital, it was clear she wasn't fine.

"Unlikely," she said dismissively, glaring at her phone and then tossing it back into the depths of her purse.

Colby cleared his throat and turned to Bob, distracting him with a question about the choice of paint color on the apartment building, and giving Silas a moment of privacy with Sarah.

"Sergeant White, I realize you want to help, but—"

"Silas." He shifted around to sit next to her, his shoulder pressing against hers, and his back against the scorching hot car. "Damn woman, no wonder your back hurts. You're gonna have third degree burns from sitting here against this metal."

"It wasn't like I picked this spot for the view." she said with a laugh.

"Why won't you let me help you, Sarah?" he asked.

She shook her head. "I don't need help."

"We all need help sometimes."

"Not today," She insisted through clenched teeth. "Look, Sergeant, I know—"

"Damn it, is it so hard for you to call me Silas? I'm not in the Army anymore, Corporal Bryant. You don't have to address me by my rank."

She flushed and wrinkled her cute nose up again. "Old habits die hard, I guess. I know you want to help, but I'm perfectly fine. In a few minutes, the meds will kick in and I will be able to get up and go inside. I'll take a cool shower to ease the sting of the sun, and then lay down for a nap. Okay?"

"Okay," he agreed, crossing his ankles and resting his head against the car behind him.

They sat there for a minute in complete silence before she huffed and asked, "What are you doing?"

"Waiting."

"For what?"

"For your meds to kick in. Once they do, I'll help you inside and check you over for injuries. If you're uninjured, I'll say goodbye and go on

5

about my merry way." He gave her a wide grin when her mouth dropped open.

Her frustration was obvious, but there was no way she was going to convince him to leave her sitting here alone. Corporal Sarah Bryant had been one of the best soldiers he'd had the honor of working with. She was loyal, disciplined, kindhearted, and she made a damn fine soldier. He hadn't spent much time one-on-one with her, because every time he looked her way, his cock twitched in his pants. That kind of reaction didn't usually go over well with the females in his unit. More often than not, it was a direct turn-off. He'd seen too many guys test their luck against the battle-hardened ladies and regret it, so he'd kept himself at a polite distance.

His unit had been sent back home long before hers was scheduled to return, so he had no idea how the rest of her deployment went, but the first half was very rocky. They'd survived hell on Earth and ended up in the same tiny town in Texas. There was no way that was a random coincidence.

"How long have you been back?" he asked.

"Two years."

He felt his eyes widen in surprise. "I thought you guys were going to be there a year?"

"The unit didn't return until the summer of 2013, but I got to MEDEVAC back in January that year."

His heart rate doubled. "What happened?"

"You know, I'm feeling better now. I think I can probably get up and go inside." Just like that, she shut down his question, forcing him to refocus his attention on her injured status. His gut told him that her back pain and her early return home from deployment were related, but if she wasn't ready to explain, he'd let it lie.

"Great. Let me help you so that you don't slip on this gravel. No need getting an injury if you don't have one." He jumped to his feet and reached for her hand, pleased when she let him take it. The skin of her palm was rose-petal-soft against his, and when she slowly stood, the scent of raspberries swirled in the air around her.

Her dark hair was pulled back in a bun at the base of her neck and her comment about old habits ran through his brain. She was right. It was impossible to give up military life completely. The fact that she'd obviously had her time cut short probably made it even harder.

The first step she took was tentative, but once she was assured that her body would hold her up, she smiled. Her beauty was blinding. She was a stunning woman, and she took his breath away. In an attempt to recover from his sudden fumble, he bent and retrieved her purse, handing it to her.

"Thanks." She accepted the large bag, and moved carefully across the gravel. To his disappointment, she leaned on the car rather than him, but he was glad to see her moving on her own.

It took a moment for her to find her keys, but once the door clicked open, they were hit in the face with a wave of blissfully icy air from inside the air-conditioned apartment. The same berry scent filled every nook and cranny of the cozy space. Silas breathed it deeply into his lungs, committing it to memory.

He waited near the door as she put her purse away and kicked off her shoes; she winced when her back was twerked in an awkward angle.

"Tell me, did the back spasms start after your vacation in Afghanistan?" he asked.

"Good guess," she said, laughing dryly. "Not the best souvenir or the best vacation for that matter."

"I'd have to agree. I wanted to bring back a sand spider, but customs wouldn't let me. No animals, vegetables, minerals, or giant insects apparently."

His playful, easy chatter helped her relax, but she still kept her distance. The apartment was miniature compared to the home he and his brother Jeremy lived in. The living room was also the dining room, kitchen, and office with only two doors branching off at the back. He assumed one was the bedroom and one was the bathroom, but he doubted she'd give him a tour.

As much as he hated seeing her cramped into the small space, he was glad to know she had a place. Too many veterans they served with were struggling to find work and keep a roof over their heads.

"Thanks for the help..." Her words drifted away as she fidgeted awkwardly. It was clear she wanted him to leave, but he wasn't ready to go yet.

"Anything hurting?"

She shook her head, "Not really. I'm embarrassed more than anything. I tried to tell Bob that I was fine, but he insisted on calling for help. I hate to have wasted your time."

"It's not a waste of time. I got to help a pretty woman and see an old friend. I call that a win-win." He moved slowly across the room, worried that she would feel cornered if he moved too quickly. As he drew close, he saw her swallow hard, and her eyes locked on his lips. The tiny, pink tip of her tongue darted out to wet her own lips, and his cock surged to attention.

As much as he wanted to reach out and see if she was feeling the same attraction, he knew this was not a good moment for it, so he reached for her shoulders and turned her to face him head on. "Lift your arms."

She frowned in confusion and he laughed. "So that I can see if you're hurt. Lift your arms."

She followed Silas' instructions, and he manipulated her arms and shoulders, and then circled to her back. He ran his fingers down her back and felt the tightness in the muscles on either side of her spine. "Have you tried massage therapy?"

She flinched when he hit a particularly tender spot and hissed, "Too sensitive."

"Hmm...with the right physical therapist I would think—"

"It's fine. Some days are better than others, but I'm tough."

He nodded and moved back around to face her. "I never doubted it for a moment. Are you seeing Dr. Keegan?"

"Who?"

"Dalton Keegan is the only doctor practicing in Stone River," he said with a pointed glare. "If you're not being treated by him, then who are you seeing?"

She flushed, and turned away. "A doctor in Austin."

"Who?"

"Are all EMTs this nosey? Seriously, I've proven to you that I'm uninjured and capable of taking care of myself. I appreciate your concern, but I really would like to lie down now." The brush-off irritated him, but he figured in her position, he'd feel the same way. It wasn't her fault he was fighting the urge to keep her close.

"I apologize if I'm coming across as nosey. I just want to make sure you're okay." Reaching into his pocket, he withdrew a card with the phone number for the ambulance company on it. Quickly scribbling his personal cell number on the back, he handed it to her. "Here's my number. If you need any help at all—or if you have another back spasm—don't hesitate to call me."

She snorted and rolled her beautiful eyes. "Right, so you can bring the happy van to visit again? I think not, but thank you anyway."

"No, I'm saying this as a friend. If you need help, call me. In fact, call me even if you don't need help. I'd like to..."—he adjusted his stance as his body responded to his lewd thoughts—"reconnect. It would be nice to talk about old times."

A sad look flitted across her features before she recovered herself and gave him a smile. "I could use a beer with a friend."

Instantly he felt a surge of hope, and he jumped on it. "Tomorrow night? Robin's isn't usually too busy on a Tuesday evening. We can have a beer and catch up."

"Sounds good. Thanks again, Sergeant...er...Silas."

"Anytime, Sarah, anytime."

With that, he left her behind in her small apartment and spent the rest of the day thinking about her. He didn't remember her being so beautiful, but he hadn't been in a position to admire the women he was serving with at the time.

He was also still married when he was deployed.

The day he returned home, his wife served him with divorce papers rather than welcoming him at his coming home ceremony, but he wasn't surprised. Before he left, their marriage was on the rocks, and his deployment just made it worse. They parted as amicably as two people could, and he moved back into his childhood home with his brother.

Turns out he and Jeremy were closer now than they'd been as kids. They had become best friends in the last two years, and recently, they'd even tossed around the idea of looking for a different sort of relationship.

Stone River, Texas, was home to several unconventional relationships. There was the Brooks family, which consisted of the four Brooks brothers: Rogan, Parker, Sawyer, and Hudson, along with their wife, Rachel. There were the new residents, a pair of male teachers who were partners in more than just their teaching abilities. Silas had enjoyed a beer with Levi and Quinn once, and they were two of the nicest men he'd ever met. Their arrival had certainly caused a stir when they took the jobs at the local school. A handful of people were uncomfortable with the gay couple teaching their children but most were welcoming. It was as if their small town had its proverbial eyes opened and was now embracing the unconventional. He was genuinely proud to be a resident of Stone River nowadays.

Nevertheless, as much as he liked the idea of finding a special woman to share with his brother, he wasn't so sure that was a real possibility, so he'd continued to date on his own. The question was: How would Jeremy feel if he actually found someone himself?

The image of Sarah Bryant immediately popped into his head. What would Sarah's opinion be of ménage relationships? Not that it mattered, his attraction was most likely one-sided. As gracious as she'd been about going out with him for a beer, he wasn't so sure she would be as easygoing if he told her he wanted the woman in his future to join him *and* his brother in a relationship.

No, it would most likely be just a casual beer with a friend, and sharing a few dozen memories. No big deal.

CHAPTER TWO

THE BAR WAS NEARLY empty when Sarah parked her car in the lot. She stayed in her car for a moment second-guessing her decision to come. She'd been changing her mind over and over again ever since Silas walked out of her apartment yesterday. She felt like no good would come of this walk down memory lane, but she didn't really have an excuse not to show up, so here she was.

Her boots crunched the dried grass that poked up through the cracks in the sidewalk as she approached the building, and her stomach twisted in knots. She paused just outside the bright circle of light cast by the fixture above the entrance. From the shadows, she stared at the heavy wooden door, feeling like opening it would reopen wounds she'd tried to let heal.

Silas was going to have questions about her injuries and why she had to come home early. She hated talking about it. It always made her feel weak to admit that one mistake had ended not only her career but impacted her physical abilities so much that she'd been forced to accept a permanently disabled status. For a strong woman with grit and determination, it was a tough pill to swallow.

"Sugar, if you're not going to open the door, could you at least scoot over so that I can?"

The husky male voice rumbled just behind her, and she felt the blood in her veins respond. Glancing over her shoulder at the owner of that delicious tone, she nearly gasped out loud.

Holy hell, he was a toxic blend of seduction and danger. In the shadows of twilight, he looked like Hollywood's idea of a long, tall Texan. Thick thighs encased in denim, worn cowboy boots, and a button-down plaid shirt with the sleeves cut off at the shoulders. The biceps revealed were massive, and they flexed making the ink adorning them dance as he adjusted his stance under her gaze. Shaking her head at her own behavior and apologizing, she reached for the door handle.

"Sorry about that. I just needed to gather myself before I went in."

His large hand covered hers and she stared at the joining, fascinated by the dark caramel color of his skin against her own freckled digits. "Let me get it. It sounds like you're headed for a firing squad."

"Nope, but close," she said with a laugh, releasing her grip on the handle and sliding her hand out from under his. He pulled the door open and swept his hand elegantly before her indicating she should go inside. "Thank you, Mr..."

"White. Jeremy White, at your service."

Now that the light shone on them both, she could see the familiar edge of a sharp jawline, and his pale blue eyes were identical to his brother's. There was no mistaking their kinship.

"Silas' brother?" she asked, even though she knew the answer.

"Don't tell me you're Sarah?" he said, with a loud, deep belly laugh before she could respond. "Well, don't that beat all. Of course, my little brother would have already bagged the prettiest girl in town before I even laid eyes on her." He winked to let her know he was teasing, and she smiled at the compliment.

"Well thank you, but I've never been bagged in my life, and I don't plan to be now." She led the way into the bar, aware he followed close behind. "I'm just meeting Silas to have a beer and reminisce about the good old days of MREs and desert suntans."

"Ah, yes, that does sound like fun. Forgive me if I bow out of that chat. I've got a poker game to get to."

By now, they were completely in the building, and Sarah could see Silas headed their way with a beer in each hand. "Hey Jer, what are you doing here? And more importantly, what are you doing with Sarah?"

"She followed me. Can I keep her?" Jeremy joked.

Silas shook his head, but he was grinning from ear to ear, "Nope, sorry. This one's not a stray. In fact, I hear tell she's got a pretty vicious bite if you rile her up."

"Damn straight," she confirmed, accepting the cold beer from Silas. "Thanks, Sarge."

Silas rolled his eyes, and she laughed.

"Thank you, *Silas,* for the beer. I promise I'll try not to refer to you by your former rank again."

He nodded. "Glad to hear it." He glanced at the other side of the room and then said to Jeremy, "Guys look irritated. You must be late."

"Yep, but they'll understand when I point Sarah here out and explain that she delayed me."

"Hey, don't blame me! I'm innocent."

Jeremy's eyes twinkled just like his brother's when he was teasing, and he winked at her. "I don't believe that for a second, and if you want me to prove your words wrong, I'll be happy to."

"Maybe later, big boy. For now, I have to fill Silas here in on all the good stuff he missed after he bailed out of the sandbox." She tried to sound despondent. Silas took the teasing good-naturedly, and Sarah found herself enjoying the company of the two guys.

They were very alike, and yet there were significant differences. Jeremy's hair was darker, and it didn't have the natural curls in it that Silas' did. Standing side by side she could see that he also had about thirty pounds of muscle on his brother. Silas had him in height though, and his clear blue eyes were framed by the lushest, longest lashes she'd ever seen on a man. She'd noticed them back when they were stationed together, but at that time, it wasn't acceptable or appropriate to make note of one's superior officer. She'd filed the fact away in her memory banks and promptly forgot it.

Jeremy said his goodbyes and left her alone with Silas, and suddenly, she didn't feel nearly as comfortable anymore. Silas saw too much, and he always seemed to know which questions to ask. She hated that.

Accepting the chair he pulled out for her, she eyed him and said, "A few years ago, I might have punched you for that."

"A few years ago, I wouldn't have done it. After leaving the military, I remembered how my mama taught me to treat a woman. It's different when we're brothers—or sisters—in arms."

She nodded, "Yes it is. Very different. A lot of the guys I enlisted with started out treating me like a kid sister. It took a while for them to realize I could kick most of their asses with one hand tied behind my back."

He snorted his mouthful of beer and laughed. "I remember that time Rutherford challenged you to an arm wrestling match and got his ass kicked. That was priceless."

"No one ever challenged me again in arm wrestling, and I spent the rest of that night with an ice pack on my bicep." She was relaxing a bit as their conversation touched on various other soldiers they'd served with and what had become of them. She desperately missed the camaraderie of the military. They'd become a family of sorts, yet after she came home, very few of them had reached out to her. There were times she wondered if any of them would have shown up if she ended up in a casket instead of a hospital.

When they finally ran out of people to talk about, Silas leaned forward and propped his chin in his hand, his blue eyes curious. "Tell me what happened. How'd you get hurt?"

Her emotions shifted, and her inner voice tried to think of a way to shut the conversation down, but she met his eyes again and heard herself say, "Thirty caliber round went through my spine into my kidney. They said it was a sniper, but who knows. Could have been a kid taking a pot shot. You know what it was like over there."

"Fuck." He said softly. "Through your spine? You're lucky to be alive and walking."

"Yeah, that's what they tell me. Lost the kidney, but I got to keep the bullet." She said lightly, trying to keep things from turning too serious.

"Anyway, I went through surgery and a lot of physical therapy before Uncle Sam decided I was healed up enough and sent me home to Texas."

She paused, staring down into her beer as she remembered how difficult coming home had been. Home no longer felt like home anymore. Her mom and dad treated her like a wounded animal, and even the people she'd called friends before her time in the Army looked at her with so much pity it made her nauseous. It hadn't taken long after she got back on her feet to realize that she needed a change of scenery. The possibility of a job in Stone River with a local attorney's office had brought her here, but when that fell through, she never left.

"How much damage is there to your spine?" She lifted her head and frowned at him, but he wasn't looking at her with pity, just empathy for her plight.

"Enough. I still get spasms that are bad enough to drop me—as you've witnessed—but they're getting fewer and farther between. They get worse when I don't get my workout in. Keeping the muscles strong helps a lot."

He nodded as though he understood, but she knew he couldn't. He hadn't been injured and shipped back like a broken toy. He'd walked away by choice after dutifully completing his service. Bitterness still burned in her gut at her forced medical discharge. The last thing she ever imagined was that she wouldn't be allowed to continue to serve, and yet that's what happened. The government doctors decided that she couldn't handle her job anymore and gave her the boot.

"So what have you been up to since you recovered?"

The question caught her off guard. No one had ever referred to her as recovered before. Everyone still saw her as an injured vet, but in all honesty, she was as healed as she would ever be, and she hated the idea that she was in the world's memory banks as disabled.

"I...um...well, nothing really at the moment. The VA set me up as one hundred percent service connected, so I at least get my medical bills covered, and a little bit of money every month. That's been enough for now. I came down here for a job, but that fell through. I'm not sure what

I'm going to do next. Just floating along until I figure it out." She pushed her now lukewarm beer aside. "How about you? What are you doing besides rescuing damsels in distress?"

He grinned at her joke before responding. "Not much sadly. Casey and I divorced after I got back stateside, and I moved back here to room with Jeremy. He owns his own towing company. The man might be a whiz at business, but he's a terrible housekeeper, so I pretty much spend my evenings playing housewife to my brother. I guess we both ended up in places we'd never imagined, huh?"

"Truth. I thought I'd spend a couple decades serving, and then retire out with a star on my shoulder." Admitting the truth to someone stung, but she found Silas easy to talk to. She'd already spilled most of her heartache; whatever else she said wouldn't much matter at this point.

"I don't remember what I saw for myself when I enlisted, but I know it wasn't what I got. Military life sounded a lot more exciting than it was," he said with a chuckle.

"What? You mean you don't miss bunking in the elements, carrying eighty pound packs, and fighting to survive with sand in your eyes?" she asked, pretending to be shocked.

"Nope, but I do miss the guys. We had a lot of fun over there. In between bullets and IEDs of course."

"Of course. Goes without saying. I miss it, but it doesn't do me any good looking back. I can't change what is."

Silas watched her for a few moments silently and then nodded as if he'd decided to accept her answer. There was a weird crackle of tension between them as they stared at each other, and then he sat back in his chair and smiled.

"Whatever it was that happened to get you to Stone River, I have to say I'm thankful. It's good to see a familiar face. Especially a pretty one."

Her cheeks grew hot, but she laughed his compliment off. "I never thought I'd run into anyone I knew around here, but I have to admit, it's been good to see you, too. I haven't laughed this hard in a long time."

"Me either. Hey, you know, my brother and I are going out to a friend's house for a barbecue Friday night. Why don't you come along? You can meet some more folks from around here, and make some friends."

She almost said yes just to see his smile again, but then she remembered herself and shook her head. "I'm not much for parties anymore. I can't sit still for too long without my back hurting, and I hate having to explain why I'm leaving early."

"Then don't. Jeremy and I will pick you up on our way out, and when you're ready to leave, we'll just blame it on him."

She couldn't stop the laughter that bubbled up, and she shook her head. "You're terrible."

"The worst, but you'll learn to love me," he countered with a serious glint in his eye that had her mind dredging up all kinds of implications in his words. "Say you'll come. I won't leave it alone, so you may as well agree."

"Okay! Fine. I'll come, but don't be surprised if your friends think I'm stuck up. That's generally what people assume when someone's always wandering off and bailing out early."

"They're gonna love you," he assured her. "How could they not?"

Pushing back her chair, she rose and picked up her purse. "Thanks Silas, for the beer and the memories. It's been fun."

"I'll walk you out." He started to stand, and she stopped him with one hand on his shoulder.

"Thank you anyway, but I'm perfectly capable. My car's barely twenty feet outside the door, and besides, this is as small as small towns get." She squeezed his shoulder, and then released him.

"Okay, but I want it noted that I protested. If my mama knew I'd let a woman walk to her car alone, she'd crawl out of her grave and beat me with a willow branch."

"Duly noted, Sarge," she teased, clenching her fist to resist saluting him.

"We'll pick you up at seven Friday night, *Sarah*," he reminded her. She waved, but kept walking. Maybe between now and Friday she'd come up with a good reason to turn him down. At the moment, all she could think of was, *I can't go because you make my insides quiver,* and somehow she didn't think that excuse would work.

CHAPTER THREE

Sarah's doorbell rang at six fifty-five Friday evening, and she swung the door open to find gorgeous boy bookends grinning back at her. Damn, they looked fine. Jeremy wore a black t-shirt over snug black jeans, and a pair of reflective aviator sunglasses, giving him a badass image with the tattoo peeking out from under his sleeve. Silas looked like his polar opposite in a pale blue button-down shirt and well-washed blue jeans. He looked softer and less lethal than his older brother, but still just as damaging to her feminine control. Her body responded almost instantly, and she internally cursed her choice of a soft lacy bra and panties rather than a well-padded cotton one. There was going to be no doubt of her physical interest in the White brothers unless she kept her arms crossed over her chest all evening.

"Hey guys," she said breathily.

"Hey beautiful," Jeremy said, stepping into the doorway. "Silas here tells me that we have the honor of escorting you to the ball tonight."

"Ball? Hmm...I'm afraid I'm a bit underdressed for a ball. You two will have to wait in the carriage while I change," she teased. They filled the tiny space of her living room to bursting, and her blood pressure ratcheted up as she scurried to collect her purse and a sweater for later.

"It would be more fun if we stayed put while you changed," Silas shot back, giving her an appreciative wink. "And I doubt you could ever be underdressed enough for our tastes."

The innuendo made her cheeks heat up, but she accepted it as playful banter and went on. There was no use reading more into their flirtations than just genuine friendship. She'd go tonight and try to relax and enjoy herself without any pressure to make life decisions. It had been a while since she'd given herself a night off.

They headed outside, and Sarah frowned at the big pick-up truck parked next to her small car. It was enormous, but it still only had one long bench seat, which would mean the three of them would be awfully cozy inside.

"I'll follow you out there—" she started to say before Silas grabbed her hand and pointed her in the direction of the truck.

"I don't think so. You're riding with us like you promised."

"But it will be cramped in your truck with three of us."

Jeremy let out a loud laugh, but Silas shook his head at her, "It will be perfect. If all else fails, you can sit on my lap."

He held the passenger door open, and she frowned when he gestured for her to climb in. On the other side of the truck, Jeremy was already in his seat grinning at her with one arm propped up on the steering wheel while he waited. Steeling her nerves for what was going to be a deliciously awkward ride to the barbecue, she reached up and attempted to heft herself into the truck. Unfortunately, between her bad back and the lift kit on the truck that put it at least twelve inches taller than a normal truck would be, she was clearly not going to make it.

A gasp of shock hissed from her throat when Silas planted his hand on her ass and gave her a solid push up into the vehicle. Flipping around, she narrowed her eyes on him, but he just smiled back innocently and shrugged.

"Would you rather I let you fall?"

She wrinkled her nose. "Maybe."

Joining her in the truck, his muscular frame pinned her between the two brothers, and she felt both squished and safe at the same time. They were such big men that their shoulders took up a lot of room, and there wasn't an inch to spare. She was brushing against both of them just sitting still. The heat of Silas's thigh pressed into hers made her squirm in her seat to put distance between them, only to find herself dealing with Jeremy's thickly muscled leg on her other side.

Blood rushed through her veins and pooled between her legs, and her breasts felt heavy and achy. Good grief, these two were too much to handle at once.

"So, Si tells me you're looking for work," Jeremy said conversationally as they pulled out on the highway leaving town.

"Yeah, kind of. That's what brought me to Stone River, but when it didn't work out, I didn't exactly jump back into the job listings," she responded.

The scenery around them was beautiful, but she couldn't think past the two sexy men on either side of her.

"I can ask around if you like. Being the only tow truck operator and full-time mechanic in town, I tend to know everyone." He adjusted his position, and one of his hands dropped to rest on his thigh, the side of his arm rubbing against hers. The hair along his forearm was dark but surprisingly soft, and she found herself wanting to rub against him like a cat.

"Thanks. I'm not exactly qualified to do much besides shoot people. I'm an expert at making beds and packing gear though." She squirmed again when Silas turned in his seat and threw his arm across the back of the bench behind her. His warm, masculine fragrance filled her nose.

"I happen to know you were the best navigator we had in the unit," Silas protested. "This girl could find her way in the dark wearing a blindfold with her hands tied behind her back. She's like a human GPS."

Smiling at the compliment, she nodded, "Yes, but only because I was one of the only women on base. Men won't ask for directions, so of course, women are going to be better at finding their way."

"Ouch!" Jeremy said with a loud laugh, "She's gotcha there bro."

A tight left turn caused her to fall into Silas before either of them could respond. She reached out to catch herself, and her hand landed on his upper thigh with her fingertips resting against the denim over his groin. Her shoulder was pressed against his hard chest. Snatching back her hand, she looked up to find him grinning at her with a wicked glint in his eyes.

"Why Sarah, were you just trying to cop a feel on me?" he teased, and she felt her face flush as she stammered for words. Her fumbling made him laugh, and he wrapped his arm around her shoulders, pulling her in for a side hug. "Next time just ask, sweetie. That way, we can both enjoy it."

Before she could formulate a response, they were parking in front of a large ranch house where a crowd of people was gathered around picnic tables and lawn chairs. A couple of kids played on a blanket in the grass, and there were torches planted all around waiting to be lit. Everyone turned to look their way as they exited the truck—her with yet another hand from Silas—and headed in the direction of the gathering.

"Hey Si, who've you got there?" The man addressing them was just as tall and nicely built as the White brothers, but he was pretty in a more feminine way. Like a Hollywood movie star or a *GQ* model.

Silas introduced them. "Clint, this is Sarah Bryant. Sarah this is Clint Keegan." She shook the man's hand. "Sarah's an old friend from my Army days."

"No way! How'd you end up in Stone River?" Clint asked as a woman joined them. "Sarah this is my wife, Zoey."

"Nice to meet you both," she said politely, smiling. "And I came here for work and never left."

"Hi Sarah, come on over and I'll introduce you to the other girls. We'll leave the guys to grill the meat while we exchange gossip." Zoey reached for Sarah's arm and curled hers through it like they were old friends. It seemed Silas and Jeremy's friends were just as open and welcoming as they were. Sarah was introduced all around, and got the surprise of her life when they explained that each woman was married to more than one man.

"So, exactly how many husbands do you have?" Sarah asked the blonde seated next to her with a baby to her breast. Claudia seemed unashamed of nursing her child out in the open, and by the warm looks everyone kept giving her, she had nothing to be concerned about so Sarah just tried not to look.

"I only have two. It's Rachel and Zoey who are the overachievers." Claudia responded with a laugh. She pointed to a big, bulky-looking blond standing near the cooler. "That's Mack; he's the older of my two men, and Ryker, his brother, is the one with the facial hair on the porch steps. He's sitting with Dalton Keegan, who is Zoey's man."

"I'll never be able to keep all of them straight," Sarah lamented. "I'm not sure how the heck you guys keep them straight."

Zoey snickered, "Believe me, they're all very different from each other. Tanner's bossy as hell; Dalton is sweet as sin, and Clint is obnoxiously charming."

Sarah's gaze jumped from guy to guy as Zoey pointed them out, but all she could see was good looking men in denim and cowboy hats. It was almost like being in the barracks again. A couple of women surrounded by men. She felt the urge to jump up and prove her physical capabilities in sight of all the muscle around her, but she tamped it down. It probably wasn't going to win her any friends around here.

In spite of their unusual relationships, Silas's friends were genuinely nice people. They'd welcomed her and introduced her to all of the kids right away. Juliet and John were Rachel's kids, and Adeline was Zoey's daughter. Claudia's new son was named Denver, and he looked just like his daddies. It didn't seem to matter who was the biological father of each child, because every man treated all of the kids like his own. It was refreshing.

"So what kind of work do you want to find?" Rachel asked, sipping a glass of wine as she reclined on a glider next to Zoey.

"I don't have much experience in the work force, but I'm a hard worker, and a fast learner. My first job was retail, and I left there for the Army straight out of high-school. I'm an expert shot"—she grinned at Silas—"and a pretty good navigator, but I can't imagine there being much call for that around here."

"You seem really young to be finished with the military already." Zoey commented.

Sarah nodded, but didn't respond to the pointed comment. There wasn't a good way to respond without explaining her injuries, and she had no desire to do that. "I came here because of an office job that was advertised. Filing, answering phones, that sort of thing. I figured, with a little training, I could handle it."

Claudia perked up as she switched her son from one breast to the other. "Do you want to work in an office then?"

"I think so." Sarah paused, and then nodded. "Yes, in fact, I'm determined to prove I can do it. Do you know of someone hiring?"

Claudia glanced over her shoulder to holler at Mack, "Hey babe, are you still open to the idea of me hiring on an assistant for the shop?"

Mack frowned and then nodded. "Whatever you need, sweetheart."

Turning back, Claudia grinned, "Can you start Monday?"

"Wait, what? You're going to hire me? Just like that?" Sarah's mouth hung open, and she couldn't seem to snap it closed. No one had ever done anything like that for her before.

Claudia just shrugged, "I'm a good judge of people, and if Silas vouches for you, then I'm absolutely confident in your abilities."

"Wow. Um, thank you. I don't know what to say."

"Say you'll start Monday." Claudia said.

Sarah nodded enthusiastically. "Absolutely, but I should probably know what kind of office I'll be working in."

Laughter sounded loudly from all four of the women as Claudia explained that Mack and Ryker had a leather-working business. Ryker ran the business and did sales while Claudia ran the office and marketing. Mack was the artist and had no head for business whatsoever. Now that they had Denver, Claudia was finding herself challenged to juggle being a mom to a newborn and keep up with the office. Hiring on an assistant for her and Ryker to share was an easy solution.

"What kind of things does he create?" Sarah asked. The reactions around her ranged from humor to slight embarrassment, and she narrowed her eyes at Claudia. "Is there something I should know?"

"Well, no, not exactly. I mean, he creates saddles, belts, purses, bags—"

"Floggers, whips, leather straps..." Rachel added, bursting into giggles with Zoey.

Once again Sarah's jaw dropped, "Floggers? Whips?"

"Like for BDSM," Claudia said with a nod, her chin tilted defiantly. Sarah wasn't sure what the woman expected from her. She didn't have a problem with BDSM, she just hadn't been around it. It wasn't every day that people discussed whips and floggers with her.

"So, is that a booming business?" she finally asked out of curiosity.

The tension slipped out of Claudia when she realized that Sarah wasn't judging her, and she nodded. "It's been surprisingly profitable."

The dinner call was made from the direction of the grill before they could continue their conversation, and they all rose to head for the picnic tables. Sarah found herself between Silas and Jeremy once again, and she shivered at their close proximity. Jeremy noticed immediately and wrapped his arm around her shoulders drawing her to his warm chest.

"Are you cold, sugar? I'm sure Rach has a jacket you can borrow," he said softly near her ear; goosebumps popped up on her arms.

She shook her head, "No I'm fine. Just a chill. I have my sweater in the truck if I need it.

He ran his hand over the bare skin of her upper arm, and then nodded. "Whatever you say. Just let me know if you want it, and I'll get it for you."

"Thanks." It was the only word she was capable of saying without making a fool out of herself. The moment he drew his arm away from her, she felt cold again, like she'd stepped into the shadow of a cloud on a hot day. It was damn tempting to lean into his warmth again, but that wouldn't be appropriate. After all, they were just here as friends, and Jeremy wasn't even the one who'd invited her along.

Conversation flowed around her, and Sarah was able to pick up on some of the Stone River gossip. She learned that a few others in polyamorous relationships had moved to town recently, and it seemed to be becoming quite the mecca of acceptance. She'd never considered that anyone would want more than one husband or wife before, but as she watched the groupings around her, she could see the benefits. Each woman was doted on completely by her men. If one was busy there was almost always another available, so there was never a lack of attention. In fact, it almost seemed like it might get to be too much attention sometimes. How did these ladies ever get any peace and quiet?

"It's not easy, let me tell ya." Rachel said with a snort, and Sarah realized she'd spoken her question out loud. Embarrassment flooded into her, and she reached for her beer, gulping down half of it in one swallow. Silas was looking at her curiously, but she shied away from his gaze and turned her attention back to Rachel.

"I'm sorry, that was a rude question."

The petite blonde shook her shoulder length hair and said, "Not at all. We're used to questions. From the random to the rude. It's part of being in a poly relationship. Not everyone understands or approves, but it works for us."

Her husband, Parker, who seemed to be the biggest badass of the bunch, reached for her hand and kissed her knuckles. He looked at her with such love and devotion that it made Sarah's heart ache with jealousy. What would it be like to have a man, or even more than one man, look at her with such adoration?

Beside her, Silas brushed his fingers over the top of her thigh to get her attention and then murmured, "Would you another beer?"

She shook her head to decline and then changed her mind. If this was a one-time night to relax, there was no harm in having another. Besides, she wasn't driving home. "Actually, yes, but first, which one of you is my DD tonight?"

Jeremy waved his hand, "That would be me. My truck, my keys, my responsibility." He picked up the can of soda in front of him as if to prove it and she nodded approvingly.

"Then yes, I'd love another." She told Silas giving him a warm smile.

The two brothers took extra care to include her in the conversation around them and make her feel welcome. She'd never really had a group of friends like this where she shared all of the details of her life with them, but she found the girls were easy to talk to, and the guys were willing to just sit back and let them chatter. Several times, she noticed

26

unusual by-plays between individual couples, and she began to realize that each woman had a unique relationship with each man in her grouping. It wasn't just about the multiple partners.

Making a mental note to question the girls individually another time, she let herself relax and enjoy the evening. The kids were all well behaved, and other than a minor tantrum from Juliet over having to eat her pea salad, there was absolutely no drama among any of them.

What a perfect way to spend an evening.

There was no denying his attraction to Sarah. Jeremy was smitten with the nervous little kitten from the moment he'd laid eyes on her perfectly plump backside at the bar. Finding out that his younger brother knew her and had already scheduled a group date for them had been icing on the cake. That is, until he realized Sarah didn't know it was a date. She seemed determined to keep her physical distance from both of them, and he was just as determined to draw her in. Like a spider with a web, he wanted to ensnare her and then spend the rest of the night ravishing her.

Her curiosity about the plural relationships surrounding them was great news. If she was curious instead of disgusted, then he had a chance of showing her and Silas that they'd be great as a trio. Although he didn't know much about her likes and dislikes as a civilian, he'd gleaned a ton of information from Si over the last few days. His younger brother seemed just as entranced by the brunette beauty and couldn't quit talking about her.

For the first time in two years, Jeremy felt like there was a good chance they'd found a woman they could have a life with. The question was, would she be open to it, and based on her innocent questions, his gut told him yes. It just might take a bit of seduction first.

The sun was setting on the horizon as they cleared away dinner, and Rogan and Hudson began building a large fire for everyone to sit around. Sawyer set up a stereo speaker on the front porch and Kenney Chesney's "Summertime" blared into the yard. Fireflies winked across the balmy breeze, and Jeremy scrambled to snag the seat next to Sarah on the glider. She held a bottle of water instead of beer now. The softness in her movements and the mellow way she smiled at him assured him that two drinks had affected her.

She shivered as he sat down, and he frowned, "Want me to grab your sweater?"

To his surprise, she shook her head, "Nah, with you next to me I doubt I'll be cold very long. You're like a blast furnace."

Laughing, he draped his arm over the back of the small seat and waved her closer, "Feel free to use me however you'd like, ma'am. It's all part of the service."

Although she didn't snuggle up the way he'd have liked, she did extinguish the gap between them, and tucked one foot underneath herself, getting comfortable. "It's beautiful out here." She murmured, her head falling back on his arm as she stared up at the stars that were just appearing overhead. "It's not like being in the city. I haven't seen the stars since I moved out here. I'm usually asleep by now."

"Not much of a night owl, huh?" he asked.

"I guess the military ruined me. I'm awake at first light, but I start drifting off earlier than everyone else." Her eyes tracked Silas across the yard, and Jeremy felt a bit guilty for flirting with her. What if Silas decided he didn't want to share? Or worse yet, what if she decided she didn't?

After a few minutes Silas made his way over to where they were, and smiled at the two of them. "You guys look cozy. Room for one more?"

Sarah laughed and shook her head, "Sorry Sarge, this is a two seater."

Nodding his head, Silas dropped to sit in front of her, pressing his back against her shins. For just a moment Jeremy thought she might protest, but to his surprise she took several deep breaths and actually spread her legs, letting him rest between her knees. He wondered if it was just Silas who made her nervous. She hadn't seemed as uncomfortable a moment ago, but now her muscles were taut, and she looked like a bunny ready to bounce away at a moment's notice. He wanted her to relax again.

"So Sarah, tell me about yourself," he prompted, and turned to face Sarah more, easing over so that she either had to slide with him, or move away to keep her balance. Indecision wrinkled her brow for just a moment, and then she shifted her weight slightly to accommodate him and leaned her shoulder against his chest. It was exactly what he'd hoped for, and he was afraid to breathe in case he upset her balance and she drew away.

"There's not too much to tell. I grew up as a Navy brat, so I barely stayed in one place more than a year. I enlisted in the Army right out of high school with the intention of making it a career," she explained.

"Why'd you get out?" He knew full well that she'd been injured because Silas had filled him in, but he wanted to hear it from her. Instantly, she froze up and grew tense again.

"It wasn't by choice. I was injured and the military deemed me unfit." Her words were curt but filled with emotion. Clearly this was a sore subject.

"You look pretty fit to me," Jeremy said, "Yoga or Pilates?"

Her eyes widened, and then she smiled, "Yoga. How'd you know?"

He shrugged, "I like to stay fit. All the ladies at the gym in town seem to do one or the other. It was a lucky guess."

"I tried Pilates, but it put too much strain on my back, and I find myself tiring out too quickly to use the weights until I rebuild the muscle I lost. So that left yoga. One of the military docs suggested it for pain management." She paused and then added, "I'm a runner too, or I was."

"Yeah? I run every morning when the sun rises." Jeremy sensed an opening he wanted to jump through. "From our place to the Keegan ranch is almost exactly five miles, so I run there and back. You should join me."

"I'm not sure I could do ten miles yet," she said with a laugh, "and certainly not every day, but thanks."

"You could start smaller than that. I'm sure Jer would cut back his run for a bit to accommodate you," Silas interjected. Jeremy had almost forgotten he was there, so the added encouragement warmed him. It confirmed to him that his brother sensed the same possibilities he did with the beautiful Sarah Bryant.

"Absolutely. We can go at your pace until you're running farther and longer than you ever thought you could," Jeremy encouraged.

"I'll think about it. Thanks." It wasn't exactly an agreement, but at least she didn't tell him to go fuck off.

"How'd you end up in the Army having been raised Navy?" Silas asked. He turned slightly, and rested his arm on her thigh. She stared at the physical connection for a moment and then blinked before answering.

"Uh, I guess I was rebelling. My dad—aka Senior Chief Brian Bryant —about had a shit fit when I told him, but he swallowed it. I think he was just thankful I was enlisting in the military one way or another." Her small, feminine giggle made his cock twitch. "I wish I'd planned ahead though. I think I could have won that funny videos show with a tape of his face when I told him."

"I'll bet he was pissed," Silas said laughing with her. "Army versus Navy in the same household. Good grief."

"It made for some interesting holiday visits, but he loves me, so he supported—" She stopped abruptly and stuttered slightly, and Jeremy looked up at her with concern. When she fidgeted, he realized his brother was rubbing lazy figure eights on the top of her thigh with his fingertips as if he hadn't a care in the world. It clearly unsettled her, but when she finally lifted her eyes, Jeremy could see it wasn't because it made her uncomfortable. She was turned on.

"Tell me about your parents," he coaxed, trying to distract her from Silas's touch. She would need to become more comfortable with them if they were going to have a relationship, but she didn't need to know that yet.

"Mom stayed home because it didn't do her much good to find a job when we were always moving, and Dad was always working. I don't have any siblings, and I never even had a pet growing up. I'm kind of a loner." She winced at the term.

"Nah, I can't see you as a loner." Silas argued, "Maybe a bit shy, but

I've seen you arm wrestling in the middle of a pack of bored soldiers. You can hold your own."

She laughed, and explained the story to Jeremy who was fascinated by this tough woman with a sweet, vulnerable side. Most of the time, he had the urge to coddle and protect her, but the more he learned about her, the more he realized that she could protect herself.

Her body arched, and she reached behind her to rub at her back muscles, grimacing. Jeremy and Silas exchanged a glance and Silas stood. "Up with you."

She frowned up at him and wrinkled her nose, "What?"

"Up. I'll sit down, and you can sit in front of me. Then I can rub your back," Silas directed. When she hesitated, he frowned and planted his hands on his hips. She'd quickly get to know that look in a relationship with Si. He didn't like to be questioned; in fact, he preferred unequivocal surrender from his lovers. How would this tough chick feel about that?

"I'm fine, just a little stiff is all," she protested, looking to Jeremy for back-up.

He shook his head and chuckled. "Uh uh, don't look at me. If he hadn't offered, I would have."

She stood up and took a step to the side as if to escape. "I'll just walk around for a few minutes, and it will help, okay?"

Silas's eyes narrowed, and he shook his head, "No it's not okay. You're in pain, and walking around could cause the muscles to spasm again. It's better to relax them rather than use them in this case. Let me help you, Sarah."

Her eyes darted from Silas to Jeremy and back. She looked so torn about letting Si touch her that Jeremy grew uncomfortable. "Back off, Si. If she doesn't want—"

"No, wait. I'm sorry. I'm just not a touchy feely kind of person. I've tried some massage therapy and it only makes the pain worse. No one seems to get the pressure just right."

Silas looked satisfied with her explanation. "Finally. The truth. At least let me try. If it's not working or it hurts more, just say the word and we'll say our goodbyes and get you home so that you can rest. Okay?"

She nodded and waited while he took her seat next to Jeremy. The situation was comical as Silas spread his legs and gestured to the tiny triangle of bench between them. Sarah's eyes widened and then narrowed.

"Have you seen the size of my backside? There is no way this is gonna work," she said, shaking her head.

Jeremy heard his own growl echoed by Silas as they both turned on her.

"What?" she snapped.

"Your backside is perfection, woman," Silas insisted before Jeremy could. "Now, sit here or you can sit on my lap, but you're going to sit either way."

Grumbling under her breath about bossy Sergeants, she turned and eased down between Silas's spread thighs. The two fidgeted and adjusted for several moments trying to get comfortable as Jeremy looked on and tried not to laugh. Finally, Silas huffed, and lifted her up slamming his legs shut beneath her and planting her on top of them.

"Better?" she snarled, sitting ramrod straight, and probably doing further damage to the tight muscles of her back.

"Not yet." Jeremy said, reaching for her legs, and tugging them up over onto his lap so that she spun on Silas's. Both she and Silas let out noises of distress, but Jeremy had a feeling his brother's had more to do with the pressure building in his balls than the weight of the woman on his lap. Once her calves were across his thighs, he patted her knee and said, "Now it's perfect. Relax and Si can put his magic fingers to work."

"This is ridiculous," she argued. "He can't rub my back with me sideways. Now he's only got one hand that can even reach my back, and—"

"You talk too much," Jeremy said, earning a nasty glare from her.

"Well, excuse me. You two are bossier than my father."

"Only when you're putting yourself at risk. I'd bet if we called him, he'd agree with us." Silas was doing his best to show her what he could do with only one hand. Jeremy could see the muscles of his brother's arm flex as he rubbed at the muscles on either side of Sarah's spine, and he envied his brother.

Sarah grew quiet, and stared into the fire refusing to look at either one of them. Whether it was because she was angry, or turned on, Jeremy wasn't exactly sure, but he didn't want to push her too much harder. Just getting her this close was a damn miracle.

The longer Silas worked on her back muscles, the more relaxed she became. Eventually, her body was draped against Silas's chest, her head on his shoulder, and his hand still moving steadily behind her. When the fireflies finally stopped blinking for the night and the fire had dimmed down to a dull flicker, Jeremy realized she'd fallen asleep.

"Whoa. I didn't think she'd trust anyone enough to do that," Silas said, staring down at her.

"Me either," Jeremy admitted. "I'm glad she does though. This—she —feels right."

Silas lifted his head and examined him for a moment and then nodded. "Yeah, it does. Are you sure you're up for this though? I mean, despite how easy they all make it look"—he gestured with a nod to the snuggling groups around them—"it goes against the grain. We'd be taking on a lot, and putting her in a bad place if someone ever decides to go against us."

"We'll protect her." Jeremy said defensively. The urge to wrap her in his arms and put himself physically between her and his brother's words was strong. "I'm not sure I could forget about her now. There's something about her..."

"I know." Silas agreed. "It's like a perfect rosebud you want to pick so the rain won't damage its petals, but you know picking it will kill it. She might not want to be with two men."

"Then we'll convince her." Determination filled his chest, and when he met Silas's eyes he saw it reflected there. They were of one mind, and they held their future in their hands. Together they would work to create a relationship so appealing she'd never want to say no.

CHAPTER FOUR

Sᴀʀᴀʜ ʜᴀᴅ no idea how she'd slept so soundly that Silas and Jeremy were able to bring her home without waking her, but she was grateful to them both. It was Jeremy fishing in her jeans pocket for her keys that woke her as Silas held her just outside the front door of her apartment. The two men smiled at her sweetly as she blinked away the fog of sleep.

"You brought me home?" she asked.

"Of course. Did you think we were going to kidnap you?" Silas teased. "Not that it wasn't a consideration, but Jeremy here thought you'd appreciate it more if we let you decide when your first night in our bed was."

She gasped and stared at him in shock as Jeremy let out a loud curse and shoved the door open. "Geez, Si. You've sure got a way with words."

"In your bed?" she murmured. The overhead light clicked on, and she blinked hard to adjust to the brightness before she realized that she was still in Silas's arms. "Let me down, please?"

He looked reluctant, but he did as she asked, lowering her feet to the floor. "I was just teasing, Sarah."

She took a couple of steps away from him before she realized that she was pretty much trapped between the two of them. Defiance washed over her and she planted her feet and crossed her arms. "I assumed as

34

much. If you were serious you'd be facing one hell of an ass kicking, Sarge."

Both men grinned back at her, obviously doubting her abilities. One of these days she'd prove them both wrong.

"We'll leave you to get some rest, but Sarah..." Silas paused and waited until she looked over at him, "take it easy. And if you need anything, call me."

Jeremy began looking around her apartment, and she frowned at him, "What are you doing?"

"Looking for a piece of paper. I'm going to give you my cell number in case you need something and can't reach Si," he explained. He found a notepad on the kitchen counter.

"That's not necessary. Guys I've been on my own for a while now. I can handle it."

Jeremy just scribbled his number and left it on the pad where it could be easily found. It was Silas who answered. "Never doubted it, but sometimes it's nice to know you can call someone. Besides, if you don't call, then we'll just have to drop by unexpectedly to check up on you."

Sarah felt her mouth fall open. "Why would you do that?"

Silas took a step closer and pushed her chin with his finger until she snapped her lips closed. The timing was perfect because he brushed a very brief kiss across her mouth that started butterflies stirring in her belly and made her knees weak. His light blue eyes were dark with an emotion she hadn't experienced in years, and she wasn't sure she was ready to think about it yet.

"Because we care, Sarah," he murmured, and then stepped away, heading for the door.

Jeremy was right on his heels, but he paused long enough to wrap her in a tight hug. "You know he'll do it. He's a pain in the ass some days."

The words jerked her out of her lusty haze, and she let out a sharp laugh instead of scolding them like her brain wanted her to.

"We'll see you soon, sugar," Jeremy said, kissing the top of her head and following Silas out the door.

When it clicked closed, she hurried over and threw the deadbolt, leaning her forehead against it for a moment and taking a deep breath. She heard the truck engine start, and she pulled the curtain aside to peek out, surprised when Silas gave her a wave. He'd been watching for her, and now he knew he'd affected her. Why else would she have rushed to see them leave?

Damn it all to hell, how did she end up in this situation? She had no interest in a love life. It was all she could do to get herself out of bed each morning, much less have someone else depending on her for something like emotional support.

Thinking back over the evening, she realized that the guys had been putting off vibes all night. They were interested, and apparently they weren't about to fight for the right to ask her out. It seemed they were following in their friends' footsteps and courting her together. She laughed quietly at the old-fashioned term, but it certainly fit the bill. They hadn't been inappropriate, even when she'd grown a bit tipsy from alcohol and then fell asleep on them. They hadn't asked to sleep over or taken her to their home. In fact, they'd been complete gentleman.

What she couldn't understand was why they'd be interested in her. Silas knew she wasn't as good as she used to be. With scars on the outside that were prettier than the ones she carried inside, she was pretty much a jacked up mess. The idea of someone wanting to build a bond with her was absolutely insane.

The last time she'd attempted a real relationship, it ended on a sour note right before she shipped out for Afghanistan. In all fairness, it hadn't been going well for a few months, but her focus on her career was too all-consuming to realize it until it was too late. They'd parted ways and she hadn't spoken to him since. At the time, she'd figured he was doing her a favor, but then when she'd returned from overseas and found herself alone in the hospital with only her parents to worry for her she'd realized how lonely the life she'd chosen was.

When she made the choice, she'd planned on it being for the rest of her working years, but ever since that one stupid little two-inch piece of metal hit her, she'd been picking up the pieces of her shattered life and nursing a broken body. Damn the luck. Three tours in six years and not even so much as a paper cut during the first two. How the hell she'd managed to step into that line of fire only someone with higher powers could know. She knew there was no going back, but she had no idea how to go forward with the hand she'd been dealt.

Perhaps the new job opportunity would give her some time to find herself. She was tired of sitting around waiting to heal so that she could get on with her life, but she wasn't comfortable as a civilian anymore, either. It was like she was caught between two worlds, and she had no way out. Some days the darkness seemed to overwhelm her, and all she could do was mourn the plans she'd so carefully laid and easily lost. While other days she felt like screaming to the heavens, "Fuck you!"

In the beginning, the military doctors had pushed her into seeing a therapist who specialized in PTSD. She'd had multiple visits, but she never really felt like she'd made any progress. The doc couldn't give her her life back; all he could do was be a sympathetic ear, and the last thing she wanted was pity.

Her parents pitied her. They hated seeing her shaken to the core and unable to find her balance again. Lately, she hadn't even been answering their phone calls because she just didn't know what to say anymore. Maybe now with a new job, and a few potential friends she could answer their calls with a more positive attitude. Something that would shut their pity off, and make them stop worrying so much.

Yeah. That was it. She was going to answer the phone when they called this weekend, and make sure they knew that she felt better about the direction things were going. She had a feeling that Silas and Jeremy weren't about to let her hide away in her apartment alone anymore. As much as the female warrior inside of her wanted to stomp her foot and argue, there was a sweetly feminine side that wanted to smile and let them wrap her back up in their arms. She'd felt safer there than anywhere else in the last two years, and that was unsettling as hell. It stirred up feelings, and feelings were trouble.

Monday morning dawned foggy and humid. Sarah stepped outside into the thick cloud of mist and cursed the weather gods for making her styled, wavy hair instantly curly and unmanageable. By the time she reached the Thompson's house, she was digging for a hair-tie in her purse and feeling like she needed a shower to wash away the sweat sticking to her skin.

The door swung open as she was dragging her long hair up into a bun, her purse dangling from her clenched teeth by its strap. Ryker Thompson grinned at her and cocked his eyebrow. "Rough morning?"

She quickly gathered her purse and nodded, forcing a smile to her face. "Yep, how'd ya guess?"

He didn't answer as he stepped back and let her inside. Claudia was steps behind him with Denver in her arms, and the baby chose that precise moment to let out an ear-shattering belch followed by a spew of something disgusting from his tiny mouth. Standing there in shock, Sarah wasn't sure if she should assist in the clean up, or run for the hills. Ryker didn't waste any time in collecting his son from his wife who was lamenting the clean shirt that now carried a yellowish stain down the front.

"Damn it! I swear I'm going to start wearing vinyl and latex just so that it's easy to wash." Claudia cursed as she whipped her shirt off right there in the middle of the living room. The curvy woman had a beautiful shape, but Sarah couldn't help but feel like she was invading their privacy standing there gawking. "Sarah, would you be a doll and grab my laptop from the coffee table? We'll set up in the dining room once I get Denver into his bouncy seat. I just need to grab a clean shirt."

Claudia's blonde head disappeared up the stairs, and Sarah stared after her for almost a solid minute before she realized she was alone in the living room. She had no idea where Ryker had wandered off to with the baby, and she was second-guessing her quick acceptance of the job now.

With a sigh of resignation, she headed for the coffee table to collect the gray laptop sitting there. She smiled at the eclectic design choices as she glanced around to get her bearings. A large, purple sofa dominated the living room flanked by a playpen on one side and a baby swing on the other. Toys and baby paraphernalia littered every surface except the coffee table, which held the computer. It looked like a children's store had exploded. Did babies really need all this stuff?

"Oh yeah, this and much, much more."

Mack's deep voice startled her, and she spun around with a squeak to face the big, blond man. His smile revealed his dimples and she couldn't resist smiling back.

"Sorry, I didn't mean to say that out loud."

He laughed, "No problem. I take it you're not familiar with babies?"

"Uh, no. Not at all," she responded.

"Stick around here and you'll get a crash course. Where's everyone else?"

"Um, there was a bit of a baby malfunction. Claudia went to change, and Ryker..." She paused and just shrugged her shoulders since she had no idea where the other man had gone.

"Gotcha. Denver strikes again. I'm telling you I've never seen a baby with such a spit-up reach. Every time we try to feed him formula, he turns into a mini-Mount Vesuvius," Mack said shaking his head.

"Is that normal? I mean for babies to throw up like that? Is he sick?" she asked, feeling a surge of concern for the small baby. He wasn't very old. Illness would surely be serious in a child his size.

"It's normal for him," Claudia answered appearing on the stairs. "He has a fussy tummy, and he prefers his mama's milk, but sometimes mama needs a break."

Sarah nodded, even though she really had no idea what she was agreeing with. It seemed safer to just agree. Following Claudia into the dining room, she settled into a chair and pulled out her own computer and a notepad while she waited on instructions.

Claudia cleared away some clutter from the table top and then offered her a drink. "We've got coffee, soda, water, or I even have some sweet tea in the fridge."

"Sweet tea would be lovely." Sarah said politely. "Thank you."

When the Claudia stared at her for a moment, she frowned back, "What?"

"You seem tense; are you nervous?" Claudia tried to reassure her.

"Don't be nervous. Seriously, this job will be the most laid back one you've ever had. I used to be a big time professional when I worked for my father in Dallas, but now...ha... Some days I'm lucky to get out of pajamas before dinner time. Be right back with your drink. Make yourself at home here, Sarah."

After several minutes, Claudia reappeared followed by Ryker—who carried Denver—and Mack who carried a little chair of some sort. He plopped it on the floor next to Sarah, and Ryker quickly secured the sleeping infant in the seat. The two men kissed their wife and disappeared with a quick wave goodbye to Sarah. Feeling all the more frazzled by the intimacy of being in their home while they shared in their personal morning routines, Sarah tried not to think about the sleeping baby next to her as she waited for Claudia to take her seat.

"Sorry, I'm just not the same person I used to be. I swear I still have pregnancy brain three months after delivery." She took her seat and took a big drink of water from her own glass before turning on her laptop. "Okay, let's get started."

In the same efficient fashion that Claudia handled her child and her husbands, Sarah was amazed how the woman bustled through business. She was extremely knowledgeable, and she had a very specific plan in place for the business. Unfortunately, while she knew what she wanted to get done, she struggled with being able to accomplish it all. Which is where Sarah would come in.

"Basically, I need you to be my right hand. I need someone to help keep track of the things I just don't have time for. You can work from home most days, but I'll need you here at least twice a week to touch base on what needs to be done. Okay?"

Sarah felt breathless. This was a great opportunity, but for some reason, she felt inept in the shadow of the woman next to her. "I'm not sure I'm right for this."

"What do you mean?" Claudia frowned, and scooped up a gurgling Denver in her arms. Somehow she managed to coo at the baby and hold a conversation simultaneously. It was unnerving.

"I don't have much experience in office work, and honestly, I have a hard time sitting for very long."

"Hyperactive?" Claudia asked.

"Um, no I have a bad back." Sarah answered, looking away. She was afraid of seeing pity on her new friend's face.

"I see; well then, pace yourself. Work when you can. Since you can work from home, I don't see why you'd need to keep any regular sort of hours. Just do what feels right, and rest when you need to," Claudia said nonchalantly. "No big deal."

"But I don't—"

"Sarah, stop. You're not going to convince me that you can't handle this. You were a soldier and a damn good one, according to Silas. Just based on his recommendation I know you're capable of logic and multi-tasking. Those are the things I need right now. Everything else can be learned."

The acceptance was complete and efficient, and suddenly, Sarah felt like a shit for trying to push away a great opportunity. "I'm sorry. I guess I'm just nervous. The only job I've held besides being a soldier was in high-school. I just don't want to disappoint you."

Laughing, Claudia shook her head, "I'll only be disappointed if you keep being all tense and weird. Think of this like a business partnership instead of a boss/employee relationship. If the business grows, we all profit. If it fails, well, I'll expect you to hold my place in the unemployment line while I breastfeed my son."

It felt good to laugh with the Claudia, even though her breast was once again bared to view, and her son was desperately seeking her nipple. There was no way to put into words how relieved Sarah felt about the whole situation, so she just smiled and began listing things that would need to be done in the next week. Even if Silas had helped her get the job, it was now up to her to prove she deserved it.

———————

Silas stared at his phone in shock Monday afternoon when Sarah's name popped up on the screen. He'd been dying to call her ever since they left her apartment Friday, but he and Jeremy agreed that she needed to be the one to make the next move. They didn't want to scare her away by coming on too strong. To find her calling him out of the blue made him giddy with excitement and shock.

"Answer it already!" Colby complained from the passenger seat of the ambulance. "Good grief. Who sets a song like "Girl Crush" as their ringtone anyway?"

"Shh," Silas hissed as he pressed the button. "Hey sweetie."

"Um, Silas?"

Her hesitant voice made his skin tingle, and he grinned as he responded. "That's me. How are you?"

"Good, thanks. I, well, I just wanted to thank you for putting in a good word with Claudia Thompson for me. I think the job is going to work out great."

"That's fantastic. So I guess that means your first day went well?"

"It was a rocky morning. Apparently, their son has a squeamish tummy, and I'm not exactly used to being around infants."

Silas laughed. "Sounds unpleasant."

"Not really, actually. I think I'm falling for little Denver. He's got the sweetest smile when he's happy."

Her tone was almost reverent, and Silas had to bite back his first response. He wanted to tell her that she wasn't the only one falling for someone, but he knew she wasn't ready to hear it.

"I'm glad you like the job, but I swear, all I did was tell her you were looking. She took the idea and ran with it."

"Yeah, she seemed a bit desperate for help." Sarah said with a laugh.

"So, any chance I can convince you to have dinner with me to celebrate your great first day?"

She was quiet for a moment and then said, "I want to, but..."

"But?"

"Can I have a rain check? My back's bothering me after sitting for four hours with Claudia, and I want to put some ice on it and rest."

Silas was stunned once again, but he heard himself say. "Thank you."

"For what?"

"For being honest. For taking care of yourself. I'd never be upset with you for taking care of yourself first. In fact, why don't I bring dinner to you? You can rest and ice your back while you eat some takeout."

"You don't have to do that," she protested, but he could hear the longing in her tone. Yep, she was interested, even if she wasn't brave enough to admit it yet.

"Not another word. I get off at seven so I'll be at your place by eight with food in hand."

"Okay, thanks."

"No thanks necessary, sweetie. See you soon."

They hung up, and he couldn't stop grinning as he drove toward the ambulance bay.

"Was that the girl from the parking lot last week?" Colby asked.

"Yep."

"So I take it she's off the market?"

"Yep."

"You're not going to spill anything are you?" Colby grumbled.

"Nope."

"Damn it. I'm pushing fifty; at least let me live vicariously through you." Colby was a nice enough looking man, Silas figured, but his penchant for science fiction and comic books seemed to deter the ladies, so he didn't have much of a social life.

"I'll tell you one thing," Silas offered. Colby looked over at him. "Jeremy thinks she's damn near perfect, too."

"Jeremy? Oh, no. You two aren't thinking about shagging her together are you?" Colby groaned. "Just what Stone River needs, another group-love moment."

"Shagging? Seriously? You're from San Antonio not England, man. And what's the big deal? If we both love her—"

"Love her? How can you love her already? You just met her. And I just don't get how brothers could be okay with sharing a lady."

Silas shrugged, "It just feels right. Like we're two legs of a tripod, and we need a third to help us stand upright."

"And she's cool with it?" Colby asked, "What am I saying? Of course she is. She gets two men for the price of one."

"You're a dick." Silas snapped. "This is why I didn't want to tell you anything."

"Whatever dude, you're the one who wants to share his woman with his brother." Colby slouched out of the ambulance and wandered off the moment Silas put it in park.

It wasn't so much that Silas cared what Colby thought, but he was realistic enough to know that most of the world viewed ménage relationships in the same way—like it was something terrible. He just hoped Sarah wasn't one of those close-minded people.

CHAPTER FIVE

SILAS CONSIDERED CALLING Jeremy and inviting him along, but he really wanted to have some time alone with Sarah. It wasn't that he was uncomfortable with his brother around, but he needed to be sure she felt the same way; the only way to do that was to ask.

His stomach was in knots when he knocked on her door later that evening, but the moment he heard her call out, "It's open, Sarge, come on in," he instantly felt reassured. She wanted him here; otherwise, she wouldn't have welcomed him.

Pushing the door open, he found her stretched out on the couch on her belly with a bag of ice draped over the small of her back. She wore a pair of short-shorts that showed the length of her sexy legs and made them look a mile long. He felt his tongue dry up and his heart stutter as he stood staring stupidly at her from the doorway.

"You gonna come all the way in or stand in the doorway all night?" she teased, giving him a big smile.

"Just admiring the view before you sit up to eat dinner."

She ignored his compliment and focused on the bag of food in his hand instead. "What did you bring?"

"Reuben sandwiches and queso fries." He set the bag on the end table. Still in uniform, he felt a bit awkward and stiff sitting down on her

45

girly furniture. Sarah sat up, letting the ice drop to the sofa and arched her back with a groan.

"Hurting a lot, huh?"

"No more than normal, really. It's always worse in the evenings," she said with a shrug as she went to put the ice away. Silas admired the view of her sexy, round ass in those snug shorts as she walked away and her plump breasts pressing against her t-shirt when she came back. His body reacted to her without any invitation, and wearing his uniform pants, the problem was going to become all too obvious if he didn't get it under control.

"Did you take something for it?" he asked, diverting his desire into concern for her well-being.

"I try not to. Pain meds make me groggy, but I do take anti-inflammatories. That helps some. I'll be fine, Si, I promise," she insisted, accepting a sandwich from him. "This smells delicious."

"It is, I promise you. It's my favorite meal the chef makes at the diner, but it's not on the menu, so you have to know the right people to get it." He winked at her and set a small cardboard dish of fries covered in cheese and peppers in front of her. "And these will not only clear your sinuses but make your belly hum with delight."

"Or misery, depending on how you look at it," she said with a laugh. "Good thing I like spicy foods."

He nodded, "I remember. You used to add red pepper flakes to everything the mess hall served."

"Or Tabasco sauce," she added. "That was the worst part about being over there. The food. It was horrible. I used to pray every day that a new box of goodies would arrive from my parents, and when it did, I'd be in hog heaven."

"You were lucky to get packages. A lot of the guys didn't get shit."

She nodded and a few curly locks of dark hair fell from her messy bun. "Yeah, there were a couple of girls in the unit that I teamed up with because they didn't get much. I shared what I could."

They were both silent for a moment as they ate and indulged in their own memories. Silas didn't know much about her personal experience overseas, but he figured it was a lot like his. Miserable, and wonderful.

"Do you miss it?" she murmured.

He met her eyes, and nodded, "Sometimes. Over there I felt like I was in control of things because I knew what was expected of me. I was the CO of my unit, so I made decisions that impacted people. Here I just sit in the bus with my partner, Colby, all day long, wondering if Mrs. Ademire is going to slip and break a hip today, or if Frank Turner is going to call about his trick knee. It's not the same."

"But?" Her eyes searched his, and he saw his own emotions reflected there, so he answered.

"But I don't miss the fear. The sleepless nights."

"The sound of bullets."

"The sound of screams, or tears."

"The heat."

"The bugs."

"Oh, my god, the bugs! I hated the bugs," she agreed with a laugh. "I miss having a purpose, too. I don't know who I am without the military."

Emotion laced her words, but he wasn't sure how to respond. He knew what she was feeling, but he didn't figure that was what she wanted to hear right now.

"It takes time to heal," he murmured, balling up his sandwich wrapper and tossing it in the empty bag. "I don't know how long because I don't figure I'm healed from my time over there."

"I still have the nightmares." She spoke softly, her cheeks turning a little bit pink. "Not every night, but sometimes."

He nodded in understanding. "Me, too. They're getting better though. Jeremy found me one night behind the living room couch with the DustBuster in my hands pointed at his chest like it was a rifle. It took him almost twenty minutes to talk me out of that episode."

She stared at him with wide eyes and nodded. "Have you talked to someone about the PTSD?"

"Sure, but they can only help me so much. What about you?"

47

"Therapy is required before they let you out of the hospital now." She grumbled. "Didn't help me much, either."

"You know, we're not the only vets around here. Maybe we should start a meeting of some sort."

"Like a support group?" she asked, wrinkling her nose.

"Yes and no. More like a commiserating group. We can sit around and bullshit and gripe about the good old days. Nothing too deep, just something..." His words drifted off. When she remained quiet, he figured he'd pushed his luck too far. It was stupid to try and get her out with people when she'd made it very clear that she wasn't much of a people person since her return from duty.

"I'd like that." She gave him a tentative smile. "It would be nice to meet a few more people, especially if they've served too."

Jubilant, he surged from his seat and plopped down next to her, tugging her over for a hug and laughing. "Fantastic! I'll arrange everything."

"Easy Sarge or you're going to be carrying me to the bed."

Her words sent a shaft of desire through him, and when he tipped her face up to his, she realized what she said and stuttered.

"Er...I mean...well, because of my back. If I get hurt and you have to carry me to bed...er...to my bed, so that I could sleep. Before you leave, I mean..."

She was rambling, so he followed his instincts and shut her up with a kiss. What he didn't anticipate is how that one kiss would completely rock his world. Her mouth was soft and pliable under his. Her hands cupped his head, her nails digging into his scalp. She was hungry for him, and the more she tugged and whimpered against his lips, the less control he had over his own response. He fought to keep his hands in place at her waist so that he didn't push her farther than she wanted to go, but she pressed against him, easing him back against the back of the couch and taking what she wanted.

It told him exactly what he needed to know, and he hurried to give her more. One of his hands went up to tangle in her hair, knocking her hair clip to the floor, while the other hand slid over the curve of her ass, squeezing the rounded moon firmly. Her hips rocked and she sighed her pleasure into his mouth as his tongue invaded her mouth, teasing and taunting her into a fencing match that neither cared to win.

She tasted like the food, but under that, was a subtle flavor of deliciously sweet woman. It was almost like tasting sin itself, and his cock throbbed against her hip. There was no way she could miss how much he wanted her, so he was almost devastated when she broke away and took a gulping breath as she backed up a few inches.

Staring into each other's eyes while they panted for air, there was a crackle of sexual tension surrounding them, and they still held each other tightly.

"Do you want me to stop?" he managed to growl out. Every fiber of his being hated to ask, but he knew he had to.

Her lips curved up slightly, "No, but we can't do this on the sofa. I don't want to stop in the middle of something because my back seizes up."

"Damn. You're right. Okay then, let's go." Jumping to his feet, he scooped her up in his arms and turned toward the two closed doors. She was laughing as she told him which one, and he pushed into her tiny bedroom. The bed was barely bigger than a twin, and he frowned at it critically. "My place next time. I have a bigger bed."

"Are you complaining?"

"Fuck no." he hissed, setting her on her feet, and capturing her mouth again. "I'm in heaven baby, just don't stop kissing me."

She took him at his word, and they feasted on each other until they were both writhing for release. His hands were under her shirt, cupping her braless breasts as she scraped her nails over his abs in return. When she reached the button of his uniform pants, she froze and pulled back.

"Do you have condoms?" she asked, her voice husky with desire. It took a moment for her question to click in, but when it did, he cursed violently.

"I'm sorry. I never imagined that we'd...I mean that tonight...damn it." He stepped back a few paces and breathed in deeply, trying to get his body back under control.

"It's okay. I didn't plan that either, but I don't regret it. If you had protection I wouldn't have stopped," she admitted. "I'm not ashamed to admit I want you Silas."

"Thank God," he teased. "I was beginning to think I'd lost my knack."

She swung at him, but he dodged the hit. "So what now?"

Silas stepped closer and tipped her head back so that she had to look at him. "I wouldn't have let this go all the way without protection, sweetie. I want you to know that."

She smiled at him and nodded.

"I know you're attracted to me, but Sarah, I need to ask you a very serious question." He paused as her nose wrinkled up, "It's not a bad one. I just...Jeremy and I have talked in the past about seeking out a ménage relationship, and I know it's unconventional, but I need to know if you're attracted to him, too. I don't want to pursue this relationship without both of us on the same page."

Silas's question caught Sarah off guard. She never imagined he'd be so blunt about the topic, especially considering the current situation. Now that he'd put it to her straight she had to make a decision. All or nothing.

"I don't know Jeremy very well..."

He nodded, but remained quiet.

"It's not that I'm not attracted to him, I mean, you're both sexy as hell," she said. Silas grinned looking too damn satisfied for his own good, "Bossy as all get-out, too. What about Jeremy? Have you asked him? Is he even interested in me?"

"Are you joking? He'd be here now if he knew where I was. Hell, I think it was damn near love at first sight for him." Silas joked.

"Whoa now. I'm not ready for love—"

"Slip of the tongue. I meant to say lust at first sight." Silas hurried to correct himself, and grinned sheepishly. "Better?"

"I can handle lust, but I'm not in a good place right now. Love would probably just complicate it more. Could you live with it if I said I just wanted to take it day by day? Maybe get to know him better before I give a definitive answer?"

Nodding, he kissed her, "You can have all the time you need, baby. As long as I know there's interest there, and that you could possibly be open to having more than one man at a time."

His words hit her like a brick, and heat coursed through her veins. He hadn't been speaking sexually necessarily, but the implications of such a relationship really became reality in that moment. If she dated both of them, she'd most likely sleep with both of them.

Two men at once? One after the other? Did they alternate or what? Questions began flooding into her brain one after the other, but she couldn't bring herself to ask them. It was almost too much to think about.

"Sarah?" he was frowning down at her, "What was that thought? It looked serious."

"Uh, nothing. I guess I just got a bit overwhelmed at the idea that both of you are interested in me." She said quickly.

"Why wouldn't we be? You're a gorgeous woman. You're also funny, smart, tough as nails..." He cocked his head and seemed to stare into her soul. "Is this about your back? Are you worried we wouldn't want you because of your injuries?"

She turned away and took a seat on the bed. "There are scars..."

There was a heavy moment of silence, and tension filled the space between them. She was afraid that he was going to bolt out the door at the reminder that she was damaged, but instead, he dropped to his knees in front of her and captured her hands in his.

"Sarah Bryant, you could have scars from the top of your head to your toes and still be the most beautiful woman I've met. The fact that you've survived grievous injuries and come back stronger, and fought to walk and live again just makes you more attractive in my eyes. My own version of Wonder Woman."

"You make it sound much grander than it is," she protested. To know that he saw her that way warmed her soul, but that didn't mean she could see herself through the same rose colored glasses. "It's a lot of exercises, hot baths, and cold ice packs. Waking up in the middle of the night with muscles so tight it feels like someone ran a bowstring down my spine. Trust me, I'm not much of a superhero then."

Concern filled his blue eyes, and he wrapped his arms around her, insinuating himself in between her knees and resting his cheek against her chest. He was quiet for a moment and then spoke. "Listen."

Frowning down at him she laughed, "To what?"

"Your heartbeat. That tells me what a warrior you are, love. The fact that you're alive and here for me to love is all that matters."

Emotion clogged her throat, and for several minutes, they remained in that position without saying a word, just holding each other closely and enjoying the experience. When he finally shifted his position, it was to run his hand up under her shirt, but this time, it was in the back, and she went rigid.

"What are you doing?"

"You said you have scars. I want to know what you're so scared of." His fingertips grazed over the puckered skin that she knew was still a shiny pink color, and she shivered. No one other than a medical professional had touched her injuries yet. A giggle slipped through her lips and he stopped. "Are you ticklish?"

"No, I was just thinking that no one other than my doctors and physical therapists have touched my scars, and then I remembered that you're a medic. It struck me as funny. I got an image of you in a lab coat with a stethoscope on." She said still laughing.

His eyes narrowed and one eyebrow arched. "You do realize that playing doctor with me won't be a laughing matter, right?"

"I sure as hell hope not." Humor and desire combined to make her feel lighter and freer than she had in her whole life. "I promise I'll try not to ask, what's up, doc?"

Unable to hold back her laughter, she fell back on the bed, rolling with mirth at her own joke. Silas began laughing with her, and before long, they'd both worn themselves out and were snuggled together on the bed, mussed, but fully clothed.

"I should probably get home. Jeremy's probably already texted my phone a dozen times," Silas said despondently.

52

Sarah nodded against his shoulder where her head rested comfortably. "Is he a worrier?"

"Not so much these days, but when I first got back, I had some trouble acclimating. I'd disappear for hours to be alone, and it always freaked him out. One of our high school buddies committed suicide back in 2007. He'd just come back from Iraq, and he couldn't deal. I think Jer knows now that I'm not so bad off, but he still worries."

"It's good to have someone worry about you. It means they care."

Silas lifted his head and smiled. "Pot meet kettle. I'll remind you of that when you get snippy over your back hurting and I make you ice it."

"As long as you're holding the ice, I won't complain," she threw back.

"Don't tempt me, love. My restraint is weakening as we speak," he said, his eyes running down the length of her body. The heat in his gaze was almost tangible, and she flushed under his scrutiny.

"Well just because we can't go all the way doesn't mean we can't fool around a bit," she offered, stroking her fingers over the buttons of his shirt. She really wanted to release them and see what his rock-hard chest looked like. She had memories from overseas of golden, tanned skin and dark-colored hair that pointed like an arrow to his groin. Even then, she'd had a fantasy or two about tracing that line of hair to the Promised Land.

Silas took her hand and kissed her fingertips. "Soon. I promise you. But I want you and Jeremy to have some time to adjust to each other and see if this could be a real thing between all of us."

"And if not?" she asked tentatively.

He took a deep breath and shrugged. "We'll cross that bridge if we come to it. For now, let's just do as you asked and take it one day at a time."

After another heart-stopping kiss, he said his goodbyes, and she walked him to the door. Peering through the curtains, she saw him outside waiting on the sidewalk until she'd thrown the deadbolt, and she waved as he got in his truck. Just before he pulled away, he blew her a kiss, and even from a distance, she could see the desire in his eyes. It matched the lust still coursing through her veins.

Quickly tossing the remnants of dinner into the trash, she flipped off the television and lights and hurried to her bed. Her vibrator was still tucked in the back of her nightstand drawer even though she hadn't used it at all in the last two years. With a silent prayer, she flipped the switch, and cursed when it remained still and quiet in her hand.

"You'd better just need batteries," she hissed at the device. Emptying the TV remote of its batteries, she quickly restocked the phallic toy and squealed with delight when it buzzed to life.

Her body responded for the first time in two years, and she couldn't seem to touch herself enough. Every pinch and stroke reminded her of Silas's big, hot hands, and sweetly seductive mouth. She wished things had been different and he'd stayed the night, but she also knew it was for the best that they'd stopped. It wasn't like they'd been best friends for years. They had to get to know each other, and that was damn hard when a girl was flat on her back.

After several quick climaxes, she sighed with exhaustion and put the toy away. Sleep came just as quickly, and for the first time in weeks, she slept well.

CHAPTER SIX

JEREMY'S NERVES WERE SHOT. Two days ago, Silas had come home from spending the evening with Sarah and basically gave him the keys to the kingdom. He'd told him that he had free reign to seek her out and get to know her, and she'd even agreed to consider a ménage. The problem was, now he had to swallow his apprehension about pushing her too far too fast and ask her out. Usually, asking a woman out wasn't a big deal, but for some reason, with Sarah, it mattered more.

The idea of her declining, or deciding that she didn't want both of them, was unsettling, and he couldn't shake the worry from his head. He'd delayed seeking her out for a couple days hoping that his nerves would settle. Instead, his anxiety had grown into something almost unmanageable.

So, when a tow call had come in that would take him into her neighborhood, he figured he'd better just bite the bullet and ask her out. The worst case scenario was her saying no, but Silas assured him that wouldn't happen.

Her phone rang several times before she picked up, and she sounded sleepy. "Hey Sarah, it's Jeremy White."

"Jeremy, hey. How are you?"

"I'm good. Did I catch you at a bad time?'

"No, I just dozed off after lunch I guess. It's good that you woke me up. I still have work to do."

"A lot of work, or a little bit?"

She laughed. "Enough. There's not all that much to do at the moment; Claudia and I are still trying to figure out how to work fluidly with each other."

"Good, then maybe you can sneak away for the evening? I thought I'd take you out to dinner."

"Oh, um, yeah sure. That would be nice. What did you have in mind?"

"Unfortunately, there's not much in Stone River. We can hit up the diner or the ice cream parlor, or if you're feeling adventurous, we can make a trip into Austin for something new and exciting."

"Oh, new and exciting, huh?"

"Yep, I've heard tell there's some new-fangled restaurants selling fish, and tacos, and even steak. I'm sure they don't cook it right, but hell, it's worth a shot, right?"

Her laughter was addictive. He could get used to listening to it.

"Sounds like new and exciting is the way to go. What time should I be ready?"

"I'll take off a bit early and leave Mickey in charge of the truck. That way, we can get you home at a decent hour. Let's say five?"

"Sounds good, see you then." She hesitated and then said, "And Jeremy?"

"Yeah?"

"I'm glad you called."

The click of her hanging up was barely audible in comparison to his heart racing in his ears. She wanted him to call. She was glad he'd asked her out. And damn it, she'd said yes! Feeling like he'd just walked on the moon, he drifted through the last couple of hours of his day and rushed home to shower and change. A quick text to Silas telling him about his date received a blunt, "About damn time" response.

By the time he picked Sarah up, he was convinced that they'd finally found the right woman to share, and he barely knew her yet. It was going to be a struggle to keep his feelings to himself until she was ready to hear them.

Tonight, her dark hair was braided and tucked under somehow, and she wore a pair of black jeans and a slinky, satiny, green top that made her green eyes brighter. She looked and smelled good enough to eat.

"Raspberries?" he asked, once they were buckled in his truck.

"What?"

"You smell like raspberries."

She smiled and nodded. "My favorite scent. I have body wash, lotion, and body mist in the fragrance."

He nodded even though he had no idea what body mist was. "It suits you. Fresh and sweet."

"Aw, so you're in Prince Charming mode tonight, huh?" she teased.

"At your service m'lady. Just don't look for me after midnight; I'll turn back into a frog."

She giggled and shook her head, "Wrong fairytale, but I get the picture. So tell me, did Silas make you call and ask me out, or was that actually your idea?"

A piece of him wanted to be offended, but he chose to push it back and respond to her question with a question of his own. "Why would he need to make me call?"

"Well, he seemed so set on you and I getting together." She paused. "I didn't mean to hurt your feelings. I just wanted to know if you were seeing me because of Silas or not."

Reaching over, he took her hand in his. "Sarah, I'm here because I want to be. It would have made no difference to me if you and Silas had no idea who the other was. I'd still be attracted to you. You're a beautiful woman."

"That's what Silas says, too, but you guys don't know all of me yet," she argued.

He sighed in frustration. "Okay, so tell me something I don't know that would surprise me."

She thought about it for several minutes and then said, "I like to eat raw hamburger with just a bit of salt on it."

Unsure what she expected from him he nodded patiently. "And?'

"And that's it. I know it's bad for me, but I do it anyway because I like the taste."

He shrugged, "I like my steak medium rare because I like it juicy. So what?"

"I hate country music," she said firmly. "It's all about booze, trucks, and depressing relationships."

Laughing, he reached for the radio dial and flipped it off. "Okay, well, that may affect the dancing portion of the evening, but I'm still not convinced to run for the hills yet."

"I'm disabled." This time, there was a distinct shift in her tone, and he shot a quick glance over at her. "It's because of the back injury. The bullet went through my spine, and I lost a kidney. The spinal injury is why I have chronic pain, and it means I can't work like most people. The government sends me a we're-sorry-you-got-hurt check every month. That's how I survive."

The emotional explanation caught him off guard, and he remained quiet as he contemplated her words. Clearly it was a touchy subject for her, but it didn't mean squat to him. All that mattered was that she was okay now.

"Is there anything they can do to help you with the pain?"

"Medication, physical therapy, counseling."

When he couldn't come up with anything else to say, he went with, "I'm sorry you got shot."

Her burst of laughter filled the truck and she shook her head. "Thanks, but I think it's a bit late for apologies, and besides, you weren't exactly there to knock me out of the way."

"No, but if I had been, I would have taken the bullet rather than see you get hurt." Her surprise was evident when she jerked her head in his direction and stared at him. "Just because I wasn't in the military doesn't mean I don't have mad respect for our troops. You served and sacrificed for me just as much as for the rest of the country, and I appreciate it. The fact that it screwed up your whole life plan sucks, but you at least came home. Lots of them didn't."

"Yep."

That was the last thing she said until they reached the restaurant, and Jeremy chose to let the silence be. She seemed lost in her own thoughts, and he was having trouble absorbing the fact that she seemed to think he wouldn't want a woman because she was disabled in some way. It was a physical setback, but it wasn't his cross to bear. It was hers. He just wanted her to let him in enough that he could help her deal with her demons and possibly show her some love.

Sarah hadn't laughed so hard in years. She'd enjoyed her dinner with Jeremy so much that, when he suggested a late night drive through the back roads and some star gazing, she couldn't resist. She wasn't ready to end the night, and even knowing how risky it was to put herself in an intimate situation with him, she agreed.

"This road turns off in a mile and a half and heads out east. There's a fishing hole at the end of it that's perfect for skinny-dipping," he said, as they barreled down a gravel road into the darkness. Tall grass—or maybe it was hay—lined the fields on either side of them held back only by barbed wire and split log fence posts.

"We'll save that for another time," she said good-naturedly. "In the daylight perhaps, when I can get a better look."

Jeremy cast her a sidelong glance, his lips curled up in a smirk. "I'll give you as long a look as you want, sugar. Just say the word."

Leaning her head out the open window of the truck she inhaled deeply and then choked when a bug went up her nose. "Ew! Oh, my god, that was gross!"

Snickering next to her, Jeremy opened the glove box and handed her a clean bandana. "Here, you can use this to blow your nose. You should know better girl; it's summer in Texas."

Spitting and blowing until her eyes were tearing up, she grumbled at the obvious. "I know, but the fields smell so sweet, and I haven't been out in the open like this in forever. I needed this more than you know."

He didn't respond, but he did smile as he pulled the truck into a small clearing at the foot of a massive hill. He jumped out as she shoved the used bandana into her purse. Before she could reach for her door he was there pulling it open.

"Are those shoes safe for a little hike?" he asked, eyeballing her flats.

"They'll be fine as long as we're not going very far." She accepted his warm hand to help her down. She liked the way he and his brother both towered over her. The height difference made her feel petite instead of inferior. During her time in the Army, too many men had used their size as a weapon against others, so she'd learned that, while not as strong, she was quicker than most of them. Quick could be just as lethal.

"Not far, but if your feet or back start hurting tell me right away, m'kay?" He peered down at her, pointedly waiting for her agreement.

"Roger that," she said with a mock salute.

"Oh, no ya don't. I'm not the military man; that's Si. I think all that saluting and posturing is silly. I much prefer kneeling in obeisance," he said, taking her hand and leading her up the dirt path into the trees.

"Kneeling? You're kidding right?" she said with a laugh.

The look he gave her made the base of her spine tingle with desire, and when his low, gravelly voice murmured, "Perhaps," she shivered, and dropped her gaze to watch where she was going.

A part of her figured he was joking, teasing just to get a rise out of her, but there was another part of her that instantly pictured the two of them naked, with her on her knees in front of him. She could imagine his muscular thighs spread just enough to let his erection point her direction, and his body trembling under her touch as she gave him the blow job of his life. What would he do if she offered?

"Right. Here we are." Jeremy drew her up a step behind him to the crest of the hill. "Have you ever seen a view that pretty?"

Spread out in front of them was a stunning vista. They stood on the edge of a bluff, and below, a river rolled slowly along. Surrounded by trees, but with epic views of the countryside and the night sky, they were as secluded as they could get. "Wow. Where are we?"

"That's the Cayota River. We're on the Brooks family ranch, Brooks Pastures. All of us guys used to come up here camping in the summer when we were kids. Then, when we were teenagers, this was our secret spot to bring the ladies." Jeremy led her over to a well-used fire pit that was ringed by large boulders.

"So you brought me to your version of make-out point?" she asked.

He hesitated before answering and then said, "Don't think anything of it. I just wanted to share this place with you. I thought you might appreciate it as much as I do."

Sarah stared out at the millions of twinkling stars in the vast darkness, and inhaled deeply. There were no bugs this time, and she spun around grinning at him. "I love it. Thank you for sharing it."

Jeremy's smile could have lit up the countryside it was so big and beautiful in the moonlight, and she laughed, pleasure filling her chest. "You're beautiful when you laugh."

"You're not too bad yourself, cowboy," she countered.

Shaking his head, he settled himself on a boulder. "No cowboy here. I was never much for the roping, wrangling life. I prefer cars to cows."

"Surely you've been on a horse?" She sat on the boulder next to him. The rock sloped slightly, and she slipped. He put arm around her waist, letting his hand slide under her butt cheek to hold her firmly in place. A flush of embarrassment filled her cheeks at the intimate touch, but she didn't tell him to let her go.

"Oh yeah, many times, but it was never in my blood. For some guys, it's like breathing, but for me, it was just something we did occasionally to beat the boredom. There wasn't much for kids to do in Stone River."

"I think it sounds fabulous. I grew up in the suburbs, so we had to worry about getting hit by a car or carried off by a stranger. My mom didn't let me ride my bike around the block until I was thirteen, and then it was just around the block."

Jeremy's grip was secure, and she could feel the imprint of each of his fingers against her backside. It was making her insides jittery and her panties wet. "I don't mind living in town so much, but only because I can escape out here when I feel claustrophobic."

"Did you grow up in town?"

He nodded, "Yep. When our parents died, Si and I inherited the house. We have an aunt and uncle who live in town, but they have their own property. I had just started my business, and Si was preparing to go overseas, so it seemed like a smart idea to hang on to it and just live there. He came back and moved back in, and it felt like that's what was meant to be. Some days I come downstairs expecting to hear my mama singing in the kitchen while she bakes banana nut bread."

"I can't imagine what a mess I'll be whenI lose my parents. They've been the only constant in my life for twenty-four years," she said.

"You're lucky," he murmured, his hot breath brushing over her ear.

She looked up at him and smiled, "Yes, I am."

They stared into each other's eyes, both searching for something and neither sure exactly what. After several moments of the building sexual tension, she whispered, "Jeremy?"

"Yes sugar?'

"Kiss me."

Once again that brilliant smile flickered over his face, and his eyes flashed before he dropped his lips to hers and sealed their fate. She knew the moment she tasted him that there would be no easy way to give up either man. They were like fire and ice, both deadly, yet tantalizing in moderation. She craved Silas's protective dominance almost as much as she wanted Jeremy's fun-loving flirtations. But could she really make a ménage work?

He pulled back and nipped her lip. "Stop thinking, Sarah. Let yourself enjoy the moment without worrying about tomorrow."

Accepting that instruction was both the easiest and hardest thing she'd ever done. Instead of arguing, she forced herself to let go and just be in the moment. His body was all hard muscle under her hands, and in the warm, balmy night air she felt like she was going to burn up with his touch.

Squirming out of his grip, she stood in front of him, pressing forward between his knees and wrapping her arms around his neck before seeking his lips again. For his part, he seemed content to let her lead, and she enjoyed the sweet caresses on her ass almost as much as the stinging scrape of his teeth over her bottom lip.

"You taste delicious," he growled, his lips moving across her jaw and down her throat to her collarbone where he suckled on a particularly sensitive spot.

"You feel delicious," she agreed.

They touched and teased each other over their clothes, never venturing further, and before long, she was boiling up from the inside out. "Jeremy, please?"

"Please what, sugar?"

"I—" She froze. Was she really about to ask him to make love to her? Just a few nights ago, she'd been in bed with his brother. Did he even know? "Wait. Okay, um, just a minute." Backing up a few yards, she gasped for breath. The air helped to clear away the lust fogging her brain, and she turned back to face him. "We need to clear something up before this goes any further."

He smirked at her and propped his chin on his hand over his knee. "What's that?"

"The other night when Silas was at my apartment..." She swallowed and glanced away from his penetrating gaze trying to find the right words.

After a moment, Jeremy gave a big sigh, "If you're feeling guilty because you kissed Silas, don't."

Shocked, she jerked her head up to stare at him. "What?"

"Si told me about the other night. I cleared it with him before I even asked you out, sugar. He wants this. *We* want this." He stood and moved in close to her, pulling her in. "But, do *you* want this?"

"I'm not sure what *this* is," she admitted.

"Us. Together. All three of us. A ménage relationship."

She shook her head. "I don't know how that kind of thing works. I mean, your friends were the first people I've ever met who were into...this kinda thing."

"But are you willing to try?"

Stepping out of his arms, she moved to stare down at the rippling river below. Her brain was a muddled mess and not just because she was craving his touch so badly, either. She had so many questions about what they wanted and what they expected from her she didn't know where to start.

He squeezed her shoulders from behind and rested his chin on her head. "Sarah it's okay to say no. We'll still be friends."

"I don't want to say no, but I'm not sure I can say yes, either. I don't date, Jeremy. I keep to myself. Especially since... well... since I got back from Afghanistan. The guys in the military see me as damaged, and the civilians are intimidated by my "wounded warrior" status. I'm not sure how to be a girlfriend anymore, and to be honest, I wasn't very good at it before...everything."

"Well, you're in luck. I've dated enough for the both of us, and I know that the most important thing in a relationship is communication. As long as you're willing to be honest with us both and tell us if we're over-whelming you, then I don't see how we could fail."

She wanted to believe him, desperately. Fear was holding her back. Fear of what others would say, and she doubted that she'd be able to keep up with one of them, much less both. She was disabled after all. It wasn't like she could make love all night long with one man and then spend the next night in bed with the other.

"Um, in a ménage relationship, do all three people sleep together?" she asked, feeling embarrassed to even ask.

"Sleep in the same bed, yes, but Silas and I aren't into each other, or men in general for that matter. You'd be in the middle every time. If for some reason that's not okay with you, just say so. There's no reason we can't make our own rules," he explained. "I know how my friends live, and they all have great relationships, but that's what works for them. Silas and I want what works for us."

It sounded perfect—and terrifying. Two men who doted on her and wanted nothing but the best for her. What woman wouldn't want that?

"Can I think about it?" she asked tentatively.

"For as long as you need, sugar." He whispered into her ear, "But don't expect us to stop trying to convince you."

His hands came around, and for the first time, he cupped both of her breasts, drawing her tightly against his chest and making her gasp. His grip on her tits was firm to the point of pain, but it turned her on. She could feel the hard ridge of his erection against her ass, and she couldn't resist grinding against him.

"Fuck yeah, that feels good," he growled against her neck. "Keep that up, and I'll embarrass myself."

She laughed and repeated the movement. Jeremy responded with a nip to the tendon between her neck and shoulder and she felt her knees wobble. "Don't!" she heard herself gasp.

"Why not?" He did it again. "Because you like it?"

She groaned.

"Does it make you hot, Sarah? Are your tits tingling from my hands?" His words were sending her body temperature even higher, and she could hear herself whimpering. "Are you wet? Do you want me to touch you? Make you come?"

"Please!" she gasped.

His hands slid down her torso and then back up underneath her blouse. The calluses on his palms made her skin ultra-sensitive, and she arched her back, pressing her breasts into his palms. After a few moments, one of his hands drifted lower, back over her abdomen to the front of her jeans where he stopped.

"Ask me, Sarah," he demanded firmly.

When she whimpered and tossed her head, he huffed.

"Ask me for what you need or I'll stop."

That thought was like ice water in her veins. She needed to orgasm so badly she could barely think straight, and she heard herself whisper, "Please Jeremy. Make me come."

Without another breath, his hand dove beneath her zipper and under her panties. He cupped her mound, the tip of his finger sliding up and down the slit. He rumbled his pleasure against her when he found her dripping wet. "Damn, baby. You're hotter than Hades. Let me make you feel good."

Her eyes clenched shut, and Sarah gave herself completely to his touch. He masterfully slid his finger between her swollen pussy lips to her clit. He teased her to the brink and then thrust deep inside of her with no warning. The delicious combination made her explode from the inside, and she shuddered violently as she cried out his name. Her own voice echoed back to her off the trees, but she was so lost in a sexual haze she barely noticed.

What she did notice was Jeremy's sensual gaze as he turned her in his arms, and softly kissed her. In that instant, something seemed to click into place between them, and she felt at home.

"I've been dying to do that since that night I ran into you at the bar," he said, stroking his hands over her body.

"You didn't even know me."

He shrugged and kissed her, "Call it kismet. I felt a spark the moment I saw you."

"You know, you're quite the charmer." She rubbed her tender breasts against his chest. The friction from the material between them and the firm muscle of his pecs made her cunt quiver, but she mentally shushed herself. After that mind-blowing orgasm, he deserved a reward. "I want to see if you can keep that silver tongue working while I'm..."

Sliding down between his thighs until she was on her knees, she massaged his hard cock through his jeans, and stared up into his eyes.

"That's not necessary—"

"Shut up and enjoy it," she scolded, releasing the snap at his waist. She didn't have to let the zipper down because it unzipped from pure pressure, and she quickly came face-to-face with the biggest cock she'd ever seen. Suddenly, she was completely unsure about her plan, and she gawked at the thick member in front of her.

Jeremy grimaced and reached for it, pushing his erection back into his pants. "I'm sorry, I should have warned you."

"Warned me?" she asked. "How exactly would you have warned me?"

"Um, well, I don't know."

He looked so disappointed and embarrassed that her heart squeezed in her chest. It would be a tight fit, but she was damned sure going to do her best to give him a good blow job. Pushing his fumbling hands away, she opened his pants and took his cock in her hands.

"You have nothing to be sorry for. You might be bigger than any man I've been with, but that doesn't mean it won't work." She winked up at him and then licked the crown of his cock, "And I'm always up for a challenge."

His groan of pleasure and satisfaction was music to her ears as she slid her mouth over his dick and began using her hands to stroke his shaft. It was obvious she wasn't going to be able to do any sort of porn-star deep throating, but that didn't mean she couldn't make him happy.

Lubing him up with her own saliva, she added a bit of a twist to her hand motion and his breathing increased. A quick glance up at him assured her that she was on a roll. Even in the dim light she could see his cheeks were flushed, and the sound of his panting was a hell of a turn-on.

As she circled his cockhead with her tongue, she felt him brush her hair away from her face, and she angled her head so that he could see her better. If he wanted to watch, she was damn sure going to give him a show. Doing her best to impersonate the sexiest siren she'd seen, she pursed her lips and blew across his sensitive dick before sinking her mouth down over the chilled flesh again. He tasted like deep, dark whiskey, musky and slightly tart, but deliciously sinful.

She had to admit this was the best blow job she'd ever given. Of course, it wasn't like she had a ton of experience, but Jeremy seemed to approve. The sounds he was making were lethal to her own libido. She found herself dripping cream into her panties, and aching to get him inside her. Without preplanning and preparation though, she was hesitant to try it, so instead, she just kept up her pace, sucking, licking, and stroking him as he moaned and panted, his hands clenching at his sides.

In her haste to reward him for making her explode like fireworks she hadn't taken into account the physical nature of giving a blow job in the middle of the forest, and now she found herself trying to ignore the rock that was digging into her right knee, and the buzzing of locusts in the trees around them.

Jeremy cupped her chin, stopping her motion for a moment, and she frowned up at him. "What's wrong?"

"You seemed to get distracted all of a sudden. Just making sure you were still with me."

She pulled back, and she glanced away. "No, I'm here. I just—"

"You're just on your knees in the dirt with no cushion, and you're hunching your shoulders which is probably hurting your back," he said firmly, pushing his cock back into his jeans. "As much as I love feeling your mouth on me, baby, I don't ever want you to hurt yourself trying to give me head."

"I'm sorry. I just wanted to make you feel as good as you made me feel." She felt ashamed and embarrassed that she'd failed him.

Reaching out, Jeremy took her hands and helped her to her feet before he stood and adjusted his erection, zipping his jeans up. Hands free again, he took ahold of her head, and held her gaze. "I've never felt anything so good in my life, Sarah. The only word to describe it is heaven, but I have no doubt that it will be nothing compared to the first time I sink into your hot pussy."

Without waiting for her response, he captured her mouth with his and drew her hard against his chest, showing her without words how much he wanted her. Giddy with desire and the afterglow of an orgasm, she let him lead her back to the truck. It wasn't until they'd been driving for several minutes that she realized they weren't headed to her apartment.

"Um, Jeremy?"

"Yeah, baby?"

"My place is on the other side of Main Street."

He shot her a cocky grin. "Yep, sure is."

"So, where are you taking me?"

They turned into the driveway of a two story farm house with pale yellow paint and dark brown shutters. Without a word, he shut off the engine and jumped out of the truck. When he opened her door and reached to lift her down, he kissed her again.

"Welcome to Casa de la White."

The front screen door creaked open, and she glanced over to see a grinning Silas leaning against the door frame watching them.

CHAPTER SEVEN

Silas was stunned to see Sarah climbing from Jeremy's truck, but he tried to cover it the best he could with a flirty smile. "Please tell me she followed you home and you want to keep her?"

Sarah's laughter had a slightly nervous edge to it, but it still sounded beautiful. "I promise I've had all my shots. The Army saw to that."

"Damn right they did. And the nurse I got wasn't even half as pretty as you, sugar." He took her in his arms and gave her a gentle kiss, rubbing her back gently as if he could rub the tension from her muscles.

"At least you got a female nurse. A lot of the soldiers weren't that lucky." She glanced over her shoulder at Jeremy and wrinkled her nose. "So um, what now?"

"Now we go inside," Jeremy responded simply, holding the screen door so that she and Silas could enter the house first.

Inside, Silas watched Sarah as she looked over their childhood home. He tried to see it through her eyes. The smoke-stained fireplace he'd been meaning to clean up was framed by a rough, cedar mantle; his father had always planned to take it down and apply another coat of varnish to it. The beat up sofa was covered with an old bedsheet to hide the stains that years of wear and tear had inflicted on its surface. All of the various surfaces were cluttered with evidence of the two bachelors that lived there. It was definitely not the way he'd hoped to show it to her.

"Um, sorry about the mess." He glared at Jeremy. "If I'd known we were going to have company I would have cleaned up a bit."

"Spur of the moment decision, bro. Besides, I doubt Sarah is here to check up on our housecleaning skills."

Sarah smiled at both of them, and shook her head. "Nope, but I must admit, Sarge, it's a shame to see your time in the Army taught you nothing."

He narrowed his eyes and propped his hands on his hips. "I'll have you know my bed is made up perfectly, soldier. If you'd like to check, I'd be happy to show you."

Her cheeks turned light pink, and she looked away nervously. "You guys have anything to offer a girl to drink?"

Exchanging a look with Jeremy, Silas headed for the kitchen. "Beer, soda, or water?"

"Beer would be great," she said, moving a jacket from the one and only armchair in the room to take a seat.

Silas tried not to take her nervousness personally. Under the circumstances, he figured she was handling things pretty well; put in her shoes, he'd most likely be having a panic attack. He had to focus on the positive. Jeremy had managed to get her here, and by the looks of her kiss-swollen lips, he didn't have to use force. That must mean she was interested in a ménage on some level.

Returning to the living room, he found Sarah alone. "Where'd Jer go?"

"He said he wanted to change out of his jeans," she answered, accepting the beer and popping the top to down a few gulps.

Silas settled on the end of the sofa closest to her and propped his foot up on the coffee table. "Were they dirty?"

"No, um—"

"Fuck no, they were squeezing the shit out of my cock and balls." Jeremy answered as he came down the stairs in a pair of loose-fitting sweats and a white t-shirt.

Sarah's face turned bright red for a moment, and then she burst out in a loud laugh. "It's your own fault, cowboy. You're the one who stopped me mid-blow."

Silas's cock reacted instantly to her dirty statement, and he choked on his own spit trying to speak. "Um, someone care to explain?'

Jeremy dropped down to sit on the edge of the coffee table, knocking Silas's foot to the floor before he reached for Sarah's foot and removed her shoe. "This little lady has a very wicked mouth, bro. As hot as it was, I couldn't stand to see her hurting herself just to give me head."

"She—you—head?"

Rolling her eyes, Sarah giggled, "Catch up, Sarge. I was on my knees in the woods sucking Jeremy's cock, and he stopped me because my back was hurting."

Silas stared at the two of them in shock. Not only had things progressed a lot faster than anticipated, but it seemed his brother was determined to keep the ball rolling. Jeremy had divested her of her shoes and socks and was rubbing her bare feet and lower calves.

"Don't get me wrong, it was the hardest thing I've ever had to do," Jeremy told him. "But I figured if we were going to keep playing, the woods wasn't the most romantic set-up for it, and besides, I couldn't leave my big brother out could I?"

"Damn straight," Silas said. His voice sounded husky to his ears, but that was most likely because his cock was short-circuiting his brain. "Should I ask how you ended up getting a blow job in the woods?"

"Oh, that was his reward for making me come like a pack of C-4," Sarah answered. Her face was still bright red like she was embarrassed, but her jaw was set in that determined line she got when she was going to power through something uncomfortable. Her words were making the blood in his veins boil, and he reached to adjust his own erection behind his jeans.

"Fucking hell. I wish I'd been there to see that." He murmured.

Jeremy grinned at him. "No worries, I plan on making her come a few more times tonight, so you'll get your chance to see it again."

"Wait," Sarah said firmly, pulling her feet free of Jeremy's stroking hands. "Before we get to that, we need to clear the air. I can't think clearly when one of you is touching me."

The two brothers exchanged a satisfied look.

"First, what exactly do you two expect from me? Is this just for tonight, or are we seriously going to start a relationship?" she asked.

"You are definitely not just a one-time thing, baby," Jeremy said firmly.

"What he said," Silas agreed. "I don't know how you feel, but if we're making love I expect exclusivity."

She nodded looking relieved. "Okay. Agreed. Second, what about protection? I'm not on anything because of all the meds from surgeries and stuff. I never restarted after everything happened because it didn't seem like I'd have a need."

Silas looked at Jeremy who looked slightly green as he jumped to his feet. "Hang on."

There was a tense moment before Jeremy came bounding back down the stairs holding a handful of plastic packages.

"I could only find three of them. Neither of us has been with anyone for a while so I guess we'll need to restock tomorrow," he said forlornly.

"Three is probably plenty," Sarah said with a nervous laugh.

Silas frowned at the packages in Jeremy's hand. "I could make a quick store run, but I'd have to hurry. The Mercantile closes in fifteen minutes."

"You could take my truck. The keys are by the door," Jeremy said, nodding.

"No! Wait, guys I'm not exactly whole and healthy," Sarah cautioned. She stood and put her hand on his shoulder to stop him as he headed for the door. Silas turned back to see her looking even more uncomfortable than when she'd talked about sucking his brother's dick. "I'm not sure I physically can go more than once. That was number three on my list. I haven't had sex since before I was deployed. I don't know how my back will handle it."

Silas's gut twisted and he felt like a shithead. "Damn, I'm sorry. I got caught up in the moment there. You're absolutely right, sugar. We'll take it slow and see how things go. If we're able to make love to you tonight, at least we have some protection."

"Silas is right. Sorry, baby," Jeremy said, moving in on her other side to sandwich her between them.

She rested her head on his chest, and he bent to catch a whiff of her sweet raspberry scent. It went straight to his balls, and he arched his hips away from her to avoid freaking her out.

"I just don't want you guys to be disappointed," she said softly.

"Never," Jeremy responded instantly. "We could never be disappointed with you baby. Even if we spend the whole night on the sofa watching television, eating popcorn, and drinking beer."

Sarah gave him a wry grin and wiggled her hips, brushing her ass against Jeremy's groin. "Liar. You'd totally be disappointed."

Groaning, Jeremy clenched his eyes shut as she laughed.

"He's telling the truth. We'd accept blue balls if it meant you were comfortable, Sarah." Silas said, jumping to his brother's rescue.

She smiled up at him, her green eyes flashing with pleasure, "Okay, then I'll tell the truth. I'd be disappointed if you two didn't make love to me tonight."

The words were like kerosene on a lit bonfire. Explosions happened throughout Silas's body as he captured her lips with a groan. He could sense Jeremy kissing her neck and grinding against her from the back, but he pushed it from his mind to focus on showing her how he felt. This night was going to be a first for all of them, and he was going to make sure it was the best night of Sarah's life.

Sarah's head was spinning. Surrounded by man-candy, she was dizzy with desire and quickly losing the ability to think straight. Jeremy was rubbing his hard cock against her ass, and her aching breasts were smashed against Silas's muscular chest. She couldn't think of a better place to be.

Wrapping her hand around the back of Silas's neck, she held on for dear life as her body zigged and zagged with every possible emotion and sensation. Her panties were soaked, and her knees were weak. Could she really be doing this?

Jeremy's teeth nibbled along her neck, and she shivered. Pressing back against him, she tried to relay her needs via body movements. His hands came up to grip her hips and hold her still so that he could align his thick cock more perfectly with the split of her ass, and she gasped against Silas's mouth.

Silas chuckled and looked at his brother over her shoulder. "Whatever you just did Jer, she liked it."

"Oh yeah?" Jeremy murmured, repeating the motion. "You like having my dick against your ass, baby?"

"Mmm..." It wasn't exactly poetic, but she couldn't seem to make her mouth work right. Letting her head drop back on his shoulder, her eyes drifted closed. She moaned when Silas cupped her tits and pressed his face into them through her shirt.

"She has perfect tits," Silas remarked to no one in particular.

Jeremy murmured his agreement and said, "And a perfect ass. There's nothing about you that's not sexy."

"You haven't seen my scars yet," Sarah said, half joking. Their instant response made her regret her words as they both stiffened and froze.

"I don't have to see them to know they don't detract from your beauty," Jeremy said, his voice taking on a hardness she hadn't heard before. "I'm only going to say this once, Sarah. I don't like hearing you talk bad about yourself. Silas and I think you're hotter than any playmate, and I'll be damned if you'll put yourself down in my presence."

"Amen, brother," Silas growled. A shiver of desire raced through her. She wanted to argue, but instead, she nodded quietly in response to their matching opinions and the sudden shift in demeanor.

They both stepped away from her, and she frowned in confusion. "What are you doing? I agreed."

Silas gave a big sigh and then shook his head. "It's not that, sugar. Come over here and sit down for a minute."

Butterflies fluttered in her stomach, and she just knew they were going to tell her they'd changed their minds.

"Have you ever heard of Dominance and submission, Sarah?" Jeremy asked, sitting next to her on the sofa while Silas took the coffee table in front of her.

She rolled her eyes. "Of course I have. It's a BDSM term."

"Do you understand what it means?" Silas asked.

The butterflies grew stronger and her eyes darted between the two brothers. "Usually it means one partner is dominant while the other is submissive. What exactly are you trying to tell me?"

"Jeremy and I are members of a local BDSM club called The Cage. We don't live the lifestyle 24/7 like some people do, but we're both interested in it," Silas explained.

"Okay, so what does that mean?"

They exchanged a look and Silas replied, "We just want to be honest about our...interests. Both of us like to be the boss in the bedroom, but we haven't attempted to share a woman yet, so we don't know how it will work out."

"Well, I haven't been shared before; for all I know, I'll absolutely hate having two stiff cocks to myself." She giggled, and shook her head at their serious looks.

Jeremy took her hand, "So you're not freaked out?"

"No, but I'll admit my knowledge of all of this is limited. I'll need a bit of instruction"—she batted her eyes at him—"and patience, perhaps?"

Silas laughed. "I can see you're going to be a brat."

"Hey!"

"A brat isn't necessarily a bad thing in the world of BDSM, baby. It can actually be a compliment," Jeremy said, and then kissed her. "All we're asking is that you keep an open mind. If you enjoy some of the play, we can talk about visiting the club so that you can learn more."

Sarah nodded and then looked to Silas. "You know, I thought you were crazy when you talked about a ménage, but now, I'm beginning to wonder if I'm the crazy one. If any of my friends told me this story and asked my advice, I'd tell them to run."

He held her gaze, but his eyes looked sad. "I would understand if you did."

Jeremy patted her knuckles as he waited for her to make the next move. They both looked as nervous as she felt, and it made her feel better. At least she wasn't the only one out of her depth here.

Rising to her feet, she walked away, coming to a stop at the foot of the stairs. They ended just in front of the main door, and she looked at the truck through the window, considering her options. If she ran now, she'd regret it. She had no idea what the future held, or if she'd be emotionally able to handle the heartbreak if all of this fell apart, but she wasn't willing to turn tail and run, either.

Glancing over her shoulder, she winked. "You two coming or am I doing this alone?" With a giggle, she took off up the stairs as fast as she could as the two men launched themselves after her. Their feet thundered up the stairs they knew so well, while she had no idea where she was going. Her hesitation cost her when Jeremy scooped her up just a few feet from the top of the stairs.

"Gotcha!" he declared, laughing as he collected a toe-curling kiss as his ransom.

She didn't even notice he'd carried her down the hallway until he was laying her down on a soft mattress. A quick look around told her they were in Silas's room. There was a flag on one wall above a military-issued pack and a pair of combat boots. It felt familiar, and eased the rest of the butterflies she'd been feeling.

Jeremy followed her down onto the bed, his mouth moving down her jaw to her throat and then her collarbone. When his mouth met the resistance of her shirt, he quickly pushed it up and over her head, exposing her bra-covered breasts.

This time, she'd worn something pretty just in case, and the emerald green satin looked particularly pretty under the bedroom lights.

"Damn, you look so good," Jeremy said, pushing the straps of her bra off her shoulders, and reaching under her to release the clasp. His mouth quickly enveloped her hard nipple, and she squealed when he nipped her. "And you taste even better."

"Hey, save some for me." Silas appeared over his brother's shoulder, and she struggled to breathe as she took in his beautifully bare chest.

"Wow," she heard herself whisper.

Silas preened in front of her, flexing his pecs and biceps. "I might not run every day anymore, but I haven't given up on myself entirely."

"Of course she thinks that good, bro. She doesn't have anything to compare it to yet." Jeremy pushed himself off the bed, and ripped his shirt off over his head. "What do you think of this, baby? Better?"

Sarah wanted to tell him no just to kick his cockiness in the ass, but damned if he didn't look like a Greek god. The two brothers standing side by side shirtless was enough to make her pant with need.

"I think if you two don't get over here, I'm going to burn up before we get to the good part," she grumbled, pushing her bottom lip out in a pout.

A look of triumph flashed on Jeremy's face, but Silas got a purely evil glint in his eyes. "Impatient brat. Trying to lead already. I can see we've got some work to do."

He reached out and turned her over, quick enough to make her gasp, but not so fast that she hurt herself. Her tender nipples rubbed against the cotton bedspread and she protested. "Hey! I thought you liked looking at my breasts."

Silas chuckled. "Oh, we do, sweetheart. Don't ever doubt that. But we also happen to like your sweet little ass."

His hands slid under her, and he unsnapped her jeans, tugging them down over her curvy hips before she had a chance to respond. Their matching groans were music to her ears, and she sent up a quick thank you for her own forethought. The matching green thong was clearly a good idea.

Two large hands gripped her ass cheeks and massaged the muscles deeply, spreading and squeezing. "I've never seen anything more luscious," Jeremy said huskily. "Have you ever had anal, baby?"

Sarah tossed her hair and looked back over her shoulder with a frown. "Um, yes, but there's no way I'm going there with that behemoth." She stared at his tented sweatpants pointedly and both men laughed.

"I don't think he was planning on it tonight, Sarah, but we do need to know these things so that we can prepare you for the future," Silas said, running his fingertips down her spine.

She fought back another shiver and asked, "Prepare me? For what?"

"A woman's body isn't built like a man's," Silas said, ignoring her rolling eyes. "Men get turned on by the sight of naked skin"—he scratched his nails over the sensitive crease between her ass and thigh —"or the sweet fragrance of woman." This time, his fingers trailed between her spread legs, finding the damp spot on her panties. Much to her dismay, he pulled away before she could encourage him. "But women need slow touches, sweet words, and soft kisses."

"Believe me, right now I don't want slow and sweet," she groaned.

Jeremy's lips brushed over the back of her thigh, and she whimpered.

"Like it or not, that's what you're going to get until we know how your back is going to hold up, sugar. So hush, and let us work. We'll make sure you enjoy everything we do; I promise," Silas assured her, shoving a pillow under her hips to lift her higher.

Giving herself over to their touch, she relaxed into the soft mattress, and focused on the sensations in her body. The scrape of skin, the tickle of her own hair on her shoulders, the heat of an exhale across her thigh. It was enough to drive her mad with desire, and yet it was stoking the flames in her belly even higher.

When Silas slapped her ass, she yelped, but it was more out of surprise than actual pain. Glaring back at him, she grumbled, "What was that for?"

"Testing your pain tolerance," he said, his eyes never leaving her ass. He was running his palm over the stinging skin in circles. Meanwhile, Jeremy continued his nibbling until he reached the half-inch wide string splitting her ass.

He blew against the wet satin covering her pussy and gripped the string, tugging it upwards firmly. It was like he was giving her a wedgie, but this wasn't anything like junior high. The material fit perfectly between her pussy lips, pressing against her swollen clit and into her wetness, making her squirm. The thin fabric gave way under her movement combined with his tugging, and the thong snapped in his hands, baring her slit to him.

"Damn," he sighed. "I like unwrapping this pretty package." Just as he lowered his face to her pussy, Silas spanked her ass again, and she jerked upwards with a hiss of surprise. Jeremy's tongue spread her pussy wide from behind, as the sting of his brother's palm washed through her backside, and she shuddered. It wouldn't take much to bring on an orgasm, she thought.

Jeremy's tongue felt thick as he licked her pussy from front to back, and then began to tease her opening. She wanted him to play with her clit, but he seemed to be holding back. Silas, on the other hand, wasn't holding back. He continued to alternate spanks with gentle rubbing and firm massage. Her ass was on fire, and her pussy was clenching with the need to be filled. Between the two of them she would probably lose her mind.

Just when she thought she was going to come even without clitoral play, Jeremy pulled back and got to his feet. Turning her head, she saw the approval in his eyes as he took in her bright red ass cheeks.

"I've never seen anything more beautiful," he murmured. "Good work, Si."

"How's she taste?" Silas asked, swapping places with his brother, and sinking to his knees.

"Like the sweetest fruits you've ever tasted," Jeremy praised. He reached out and turned her onto her back, giving her a hard kiss. She'd never tasted herself before, but the flavor was slightly intoxicating. She didn't know if it was because she was so turned on, or because it was via Jeremy's mouth, but she wasn't complaining.

Beside the bed, Silas lifted her legs so that they were draped over his broad shoulders, and he gripped her thighs tightly. His technique was very different from Jeremy's. He was more carnal and significantly rougher, but she found that after Jeremy's gentle touches building her up, she needed Silas's harder strokes.

Jeremy took a nipple in his mouth and bit down just as Silas sucked her clit into his mouth. She shattered without warning. Her body convulsed against them, pussy clenching and creaming as she cried out. Stars flickered behind her eyelids, but she was pleased to feel no pain in her back at all. Maybe this would work out better than she'd hoped.

When her brain finally began firing again, she realized that the two men had finished stripping their clothes off and crawled into bed on either side of her. They were lazily stroking her body, and even after two phenomenal orgasms in less than two hours, she was feeling the desire rekindle.

"Wow," she whispered.

"That was beautiful," Silas said, giving her a sweet kiss. She tasted herself on his lips and determined that that flavor was slightly different with each brother. Attributing it to their unique flavors, she decided that both were deliciously addictive.

"It was pretty freaking awesome on this end, too," she agreed.

Laughing, Jeremy tweaked her nipple. "Did we wear you out?"

"Depends on what you've got in mind. I'm not sure I'm up for PT, but I could use a deep tissue massage right about now," she teased.

"Oh I'll massage you deep, baby," he said, his clear blue eyes sparkling with mischief. "But you're going to take Si first. I don't want to hurt you."

The sacrifice touched her. She'd wondered how they would figure out who went first, but to have Jeremy give that moment up for her sake meant the world to her. Turning, she drew his face to hers and kissed him deeply.

"You're one in a million, cowboy," she said against his lips.

"A trillion, but who's counting?" he joked.

Silas nipped her shoulder, and she turned her attention to him. "Are you sure you're okay, Sarah?"

"Perfect," she said, honestly. "Never been better."

"I just don't want to do anything that might—"

"Hurt me. Yeah, I got it, Sarge. I'm not a china doll. Now shut your trap and make love to me before your brother beats you to it."

Her pleasure at his grumble of annoyance was short-lived because he didn't let her take control for a moment. Rolling her to her back, he slid between her thighs and pushed his fingers into her tight passage, stretching her as he sucked on her nipples.

When Jeremy passed his older brother a condom, she had a second of hesitation before she rationalized the situation in her head. She wanted this. More than she wanted anything else, she wanted to feel Silas inside of her. To hear him call out her name when he exploded with passion. Giving him her most seductive smile, she snatched the condom, and tore it open with her teeth.

When she began sliding it over his cock, he hissed in pleasure, but he didn't stop her. Guiding him to her opening, she put his cockhead in place and then whispered, "Please, Silas?"

The time it took for him to slide home was shorter than a breath, and she felt the sting of her muscles stretching wide throughout her entire body. It was exhilarating. Clenching her muscles down on him, she could feel her own pussy greedily grabbing at his cock as if to hold it in place. His thrusts were slow and steady for the first few minutes, then he changed positions, rising up onto his knees, and lifting her ass. Suddenly, he was thrusting right against the perfect spot inside her cunt, and she began twitching and trembling as her body reached for yet another orgasm.

The more she tried to press down, the harder his hands gripped her hips to hold her up, and she grew frantic with need. "Silas, please! I need to come."

"Ask for it, sugar," he instructed.

"Please make me come." Her words were mostly clear, but she was having trouble focusing. Fire burned through her body making her mindless with need. "Please, please!"

One more thrust was all she needed to fly over the cliff and into oblivion. The moment her body clenched down on his, he exploded inside her.

He roared when he came, his body jerking against her, and his cock jumping inside her. She would most likely have bruises where his thumbs dug into her hipbones to hold her in place, but she didn't care. All that mattered was the fireworks exploding throughout her body. She'd finally achieved nirvana.

———————

Jeremy had never seen anything so damned erotic in his life. Watching Silas make Sarah shatter with an orgasm really did it for him. He wanted to be in his brother's place, and he wanted to watch them go again. It was mind-boggling.

His cock was screaming with need, but he held it tightly at the base, refusing to give up his control. When he came, he was going to be deep inside of her; that was for damn sure.

Covering himself with a condom, he waited patiently for Silas to roll to the side. Sarah followed his warmth instinctively turning her back to Jeremy, and he took advantage of it. Sliding in behind her, he lifted her thigh and pressed the head of his cock into her dripping opening. Between orgasms and sex she was relaxed enough that he was able to ease into her with only a few short thrusts.

The moment he was balls-deep inside of her, he felt tears of emotion sting his eyes. It was like something clicked inside of him, and his whole life fell into place. This was his woman. Whether she knew it or not, he'd never be able to survive without her again.

Unlike Silas's noisy fucking, Jeremy made love to Sarah slowly, and quietly. He drew her back to climax with him by stroking her clit from behind. When he came deep inside of her, his only regret was that he wasn't filling her with his cum. It would be monumental when he did that, but it would have to wait. Sarah wasn't ready for that yet.

He and Silas worked together to clean her up after their love-making because she'd promptly fallen asleep after her third orgasm. After a quick shower, Jeremy joined the two of them in the bed, pulling Sarah into his arms so that her head rested on his shoulder. Silas draped his arm over her waist, and together, the three of them slept.

CHAPTER EIGHT

Two BLISSFUL WEEKS had passed since Sarah's first night with the White brothers, and she was beginning to feel almost human again. Between working every day with Claudia and spending her evenings with Silas and Jeremy, it seemed like her life was finding a happy cadence.

Years in the military had created a need for structure in her life, so she'd plotted specific hours to work from home and appointed times to be at the Thompson's house. It made her feel necessary again when Claudia called on her for answers or asked her for help. Her sense of gratification increased as Ryker began doling out projects to her as well. The system appeared to be working well for all of them, and she was really beginning to understand the art behind their creations, too. Mack had an amazing skill that she both admired and envied. Under his hands, a piece of plain brown leather took on a glossy sheen and a whole new life.

After spending a few hours in his shop watching him work, she'd voiced her awe at his talent, and he offered to teach her a few tricks of the trade. Holding the rough leather in her hands while applying tools to it gave new meaning to the world. She'd gone from feeling useless and broken, to creating something beautiful. Of course, her neatly tooled piece of leather had absolutely no purpose yet, but she loved it anyway.

Mack had given her permission to use the shop in her off hours and promised her more lessons as time permitted.

Outside of her newfound work life, her personal life was in a continual state of hazy lust. It seemed like the moment she got within arm's reach of one of her men she was aching with desire. Neither man complained, though; in fact, the feeling seemed to be mutual. They could barely keep their hands off each other. There had been a few mishaps with her back, but mostly, the only parts of her that ached were the ones that were being well used.

The horror on Jeremy's face when her back spasmed in the middle of a change in position was a harsh reminder that she wasn't a fully capable woman. She'd never be able to go for hours on end without rest, and there were some positions that she'd most likely never be comfortable in. Thankfully, neither guy seemed to mind too much. She wasn't naïve enough to believe that everything would remain picture perfect, but at least she finally felt hopeful.

Juggling a box full of donuts, her laptop bag, and her purse, she cursed when her back tightened up as she twisted to get up out of the car. Hanging in limbo with her elbows on the door frame and her lower body unwilling to cooperate any further, she ran through the options in her mind.

She could collapse back into the seat, but that would result in the donuts or the laptop hitting the dirt, and she didn't want to sacrifice either. Alternately, she could attempt to force her back into a vertical position which could result in agonizing pain and the possibility of a complete blackout...in which case everything—including her—would hit the dirt. Finally, she settled on option C, and yelled as loud as possible.

"Claudia!" After a pause she tried again, "Claudia! Mack! Anyone?"

The front door swung open and Mack pushed through followed closely by Claudia and Ryker who was carrying Denver.

"What's wrong?" Claudia asked as she came down the porch steps.

"My back," Sarah panted. "It seized up." She instinctively started to rise up as Mack drew closer and gasped at the pain.

"Don't move," Mack snapped, reaching out to empty her arms, blissfully lightening the pressure.

"Do I need to call 911?" Ryker called out. Denver whimpered at the concern in his father's tone, and Sarah silently cursed her situation again.

"No, I just needed a bit of help," she answered. Mack put one arm around her waist and helped her move out of the doorway so that Claudia could shut the door. "I'm sorry to scare you guys."

"Don't be," Mack said shortly, "What do you need us to do? Do you want to go inside, or do we need to bring a chair out here for you?"

The kindness in his tone, and the absolute security she felt with him touching her was emotionally moving. She hadn't even felt the need to pull away when he touched her. How long had it been since she'd been comfortable with being touched? Clearly, Silas and Jeremy were having an impact on her.

"If you can help me in to the couch, I just need to sit and let the muscles relax. I have some medication in my purse that will help. This happens sometimes when I move wrong," she explained.

Claudia moved to her other side, and between the two of them, they helped her up the steps and into the house with minimal discomfort. Once she was situated on the sofa, Claudia got her a glass of tea and sat down next to her with a sigh of relief.

"That was exciting," she commented, and Sarah laughed.

"If you find that exciting, you really need to get out more."

Shrugging, Claudia smiled. "Hey, I'm at home all day with an infant. My only source of entertainment is my husbands. Occasionally, it's nice to have something out of the ordinary."

"Well I'm glad I could help out."

Ryker peered at her curiously. "How long has your back been like that?"

"Since the surgeon pulled a bullet and a kidney out," she joked. When no one laughed, she sighed, "It's getting better. I've been pushing it a bit in the last couple of weeks. I just need to rest it."

"I'm going to guess the White brothers have had a hand in your recent increase in activity level," Mack observed. She felt her face flush, and she looked away. "Does Silas know you're having trouble?"

"I'm not having trouble, I swear. This was just a one-time thing. I twisted wrong as I got out of the car because my hands were full." She groaned. "Damn it. The donuts are still on top of the car."

"Donuts?" Ryker asked, perking up and glancing at the front door. "I'll go get them."

"You brought donuts?" Mack smiled at his brother's abrupt exit. He reached down and turned on the vibrating chair that Denver occupied. "One time or not, you still need to tell Si."

"Yes, I brought donuts, and I'm not going to worry him over nothing, but thank you for being concerned. I'm feeling better just sitting here."

Mack seemed to consider pushing her, but then thought better of it. Rising, he kissed his wife on the forehead. "Okay, if you need me, I'll be at the workshop. I'm going to snag myself a donut before Ryker eats them all. See you later, sweetheart."

Reappearing in the doorway a moment later with the box of donuts and powdered sugar smile, Ryker thanked her for the treat and kissed his wife goodbye, leaving them alone to talk.

"So you're officially dating Silas and Jeremy, huh?" Claudia asked point blank.

Feeling uncomfortable about discussing her personal life with her boss, she just nodded.

"You know I'm married to two men, right? I mean, if you're worried about being judged, you shouldn't be."

Sarah gave her a small smile, "We just haven't exactly put a label on what we have. I'm not sure what's going to happen."

"But you are seeing them both?"

"Yeah."

Claudia's face bloomed into a smile, "Awesome. You're perfect for them."

"I am?"

"Absolutely! You've got fire in your veins and a strong spirit. Those two need a woman who can keep them in line."

Snorting, Sarah shook her head. "I don't know about that. Lately, my blood has been more water and less fire."

"That's just because you've been feeling sorry for yourself," Claudia said thoughtfully. "You know what I see when I look at you?"

Sarah gave her a wary glance. "What?"

"A bitch." Claudia laughed when Sarah's mouth fell open. "I mean that in the nicest possible way."

"How can being a bitch be a good thing?"

"You seem like a tough girl, like you'd do anything to prove you're as strong and as badass as the men around you." Claudia paused, and Sarah nodded. "You probably had to fight for respect your whole life because you moved with your family so much. Then, when you got in the military, you had to prove yourself. I can only imagine how hard it is to be a woman in the military."

"It wasn't all bad," Sarah said noncommittally. She could see where Claudia was going with her train of thought, but she wasn't quite ready to accept the term bitch yet.

"In my mind, a woman who has to harden her exterior to protect her heart has put on the persona of a bitch. I don't truly think you are that person inside, but on the outside, you come across as defensive, and—" Claudia broke off, and looked away suddenly.

"Don't stop there; tell me how you really feel," Sarah snarked.

"See, that's what I mean. You can be a woman and still be tough as nails. You can have friends, have lovers, hell, you can even have a heart. You've been working for me for three weeks, and I like to think—and I hope you think—that we're friends. I'm telling you as your friend, you need to work on letting people in. Stop being such a stubborn ass, and let people like you."

"Wow." Sarah stared into space for a moment, digesting Claudia's words. "All of that because I didn't want to tell Silas about my back."

"No, I've been wanting to say it for a while now, but I hadn't found the right opportunity. I like you a lot Sarah, and I really want us to be good friends. I think you've found two men who will treat you like a queen if you'll let them, but you have to see yourself as worthy."

"Worthy?"

"Yeah, stop thinking of yourself as not good enough. Stop trying to prove something."

"I don't know if I can." Sarah finally admitted.

"No worries, I broke Ryker; I can surely break you down," Claudia teased with a wink. "Now, how is your back?"

"Much better."

"Good, let me grab my laptop and we'll work from here while Denver is napping. Later we can have a good gossipfest about what the guys are like in bed." She wiggled her eyebrows and Sarah laughed.

"Amazing, of course," she answered.

"Uh huh, but I want details, woman."

By the time Sarah headed for home later that afternoon, she was feeling great. She was overjoyed to realize she truly did have a friend in Claudia. Sure, the woman was blunt, but she was also honest, and Sarah appreciated that.

Most likely, she was right in her assumptions, too. After decades of trying to prove herself worthy, she'd been injured overseas and suddenly labeled disabled. That damaged her mentally more than physically even. Somehow, she had to move on and let it go.

Rushing around her apartment doing some last minute cleaning before the guys arrived with take-out for an evening in, she was startled by a soft knock on her door. A peek out the window made her stomach flip-flop, and she hesitated.

"Sarah? I know you're in there. I saw the curtains move. Open the door, honey."

Heart racing, she gripped the door knob and considered her options. She could either ignore her mother's plea, or open the door and face her pity. Neither was a great option because her mother was nothing if not tenacious. Sarah wouldn't put it past Olivia to call the authorities and ask them to bust down the door and check on her. No, there was no way to avoid this face-off, but she'd be damned if it would last long.

Flinging the door open, she frowned at her mother. "Hi, Mom."

"Hello, Sarah. I'm glad to see you up and moving around. Have you been doing those exercises?" Olivia Bryant shared her daughter's curvy build, and it had been a point of contention between the two of them for years. Sarah might be curvy, but she was very healthy. The Army had seen to that. Olivia preferred to enhance her curves with waist trainers and low carb diets that made her narrow waist seem almost sickeningly thin.

"Yes, Mom, I'm doing just fine. In fact I'm doing great. Is that all you came down here for?"

A flash of hurt in her mother's eyes made Sarah bite her tongue before she said anything more. Sarah might not agree with everything her mother did, but there was no doubt she loved her. Her parents were over-protective but they'd done their best, and she was grateful for the life they'd given her.

"I'm sorry; I'm just in a hurry. I have company coming over soon..."

Olivia's eyes widened. "Oh, that's wonderful, honey. I'm so glad you're making friends down here. I was concerned when you moved. I mean, you've always been a bit more introverted, but after you came home from the hospital, you just seemed so shut off from everything."

"Yeah, well, I'm not anymore. I have a job, and I'm doing just fine. You and Daddy can quit worrying about me." She gestured to the apartment around her.

"That's not likely to happen anytime soon. You're our child, Sarah. We'll always worry about you." The love on her mother's face warmed her heart, and she returned Olivia's smile.

"I know, Mom. I love you, too. So tell me, what brought you all the way to Stone River? And where's Daddy?"

"Your father thought it best that he stay home this time. He was very upset after your last conversation, and you haven't been answering my calls." Olivia settled on the sofa and patted the seat next to her. Sighing, Sarah joined her. "Honey, I'm not sure why you're so angry with us. We just want to help."

"No, you want to take care of me."

"What's so wrong with that?"

"I'm disabled, but I'm not an invalid," she snapped, huffing with frustration.

"We know that, but you're dealing with very serious injuries, Sarah. It's not like you scraped your knee and we wrapped you in cotton. For God's sake, you nearly died!" Olivia's green eyes, so like her own, were filled with the sheen of tears, and Sarah's anger fizzled out of her. She could only imagine the hell her parents went through when she was shot. Getting that phone call was every family's worst nightmare.

"I know, Mom. I just needed some space." She hugged her mom close. "And look at how good it's been for me."

She pulled back when Olivia stiffened in her arms. "It looks to me like you're having a much nicer time than I thought. Hello, gentlemen."

Sarah turned to see Silas and Jeremy standing in the doorway, looking embarrassed to be there. Inwardly groaning, she debated whether or not to introduce them, or ask them to leave. She wasn't sure she was ready to spill the beans about her three-way relationship just yet.

"Uh, hi guys. Mom, this is Silas and Jeremy White. Silas and I are old friends. We actually served together." Sarah said jumped to her feet and gave the guys a very pointed look she hoped they understood.

"Mrs. Bryant, it's nice to meet you," Silas said with a nod.

Jeremy—ever the easygoing one—grinned cheerfully and took her mom in a bear hug. "I can see where Sarah gets her good looks. Any chance that's Miz Bryant instead of Missus?"

Olivia giggled like a school girl and batted his arms away. "Pfft. Last I checked, Mr. Bryant still called me Missus."

"Damn, guess I'll have to keep charming your pretty daughter then." He winked at Sarah and then turned back to Olivia.

Sarah frowned at her mother who smiled widely, her eyes filling with joy. "Are you two dating then?"

"Uh, guys can I speak with you for just a moment, outside?" Sarah said, emphasizing her words with a jerk of her head.

The two men followed her out onto the sidewalk, shutting her mother in her apartment and giving them a tiny bit of privacy. The moment she heard the latch click she shook her head at them, "We can't tell her."

Silas frowned, "Why not?"

"Because she won't understand. My mom and dad are from a different era. They're very conservative. Besides, they still think of me as their little girl. What do you think my Dad will do when he finds out you two are boning his baby?"

"Boning." Jeremy laughed, and hugged her. "Man, I love you."

Sarah instantly froze, all of the blood draining to her toes as shock washed over her. "What?"

"I love you, baby," he said, kissing her lightly. "If you need more time before we tell your parents, it's no problem."

"Yes, it is a problem. It's lying by omission," Silas grumbled.

"It's not lying. It's just not filling them in on all of the details," Jeremy argued. "Besides, it's not like we'll never tell them. Hell, they'll figure it out when there are two grooms at the altar."

Sarah's knees rocked underneath her, and if not for Jeremy's strong arms, she would have fallen to the ground. When did they move from dating to planning a wedding? Her brain was foggy, but she knew enough to send them home.

"Can I just call you guys later? I didn't know she was coming, and I'm not sure yet what she wants, but I need to spend time with her. Okay?"

Jeremy kissed her forehead, and said, "Of course, baby. Call us before you go to sleep. We can try out some phone sex." He wiggled his eyebrows, and she laughed in spite of her anxiety.

Silas finally nodded in agreement and hugged her tight. "Promise me you'll tell her the truth?"

"I'll think about it."

"And we're going to talk more about this later, sugar. I think the three of us need to get some things straight," he said, making her stomach twist even more. That was the last thing she wanted to do. Talking meant admitting things she'd yet to even acknowledge to herself. She wasn't ready for talking, but she nodded in order to get him to let her go.

She waited until both of them were in the truck and backing out before she went back into the apartment to face her mother.

Olivia was standing near the window with a thoughtful expression on her face, and Sarah groaned loudly. "You were spying on us, weren't you?"

"Spying is such a harsh term."

"Mom!"

"If you're asking me whether or not I saw you hugging and kissing on both of those handsome men, then the answer is yes, but I must admit to being a bit confused by you sending them away. Did you not want me to meet your boyfriends?" Hurt was evident on Olivia's face, but shock was all Sarah was feeling.

"Um, they're not exactly, well, I mean, it's still really new, and..." She shook her head to clear away the surprise and started over. "You don't care that there are two of them?"

Olivia laughed. "Why would I care? If they make you happy then they make me happy. I'm a bit confused about how it works, but I'm sure you can fill in the blanks for me." She paused but Sarah couldn't think of anything to say in response. She'd been so sure that her mother would hate the idea. "What is that look for, Sarah?"

"I just thought, I mean you've always been so judgmental of my choices that I just assumed you'd hate this one, too."

Dropping heavily on the sofa Olivia looked like she'd been slapped. "Judgmental? Is that how you see me?"

"I'm sorry. It's just, with the comments about my weight, and you were disappointed when I enlisted, and you hated that I wanted to go to sniper school in the future."

Shaking her head, Olivia began to cry. "I never realized... Sarah, I love you more than life itself. I never meant to make you feel bad about yourself or your choices."

"I know I'm not the daughter you hoped, mom. I'm not girly, or feminine, and now I'm not even able to be a soldier." Tears slid down her cheeks as she sat next to her mom and they hugged tightly.

"No, you're not the daughter I hoped for, because you're better than I ever could have imagined! Do you know how proud I am of you? When you were overseas I told everyone I knew about you and what you were doing, and when you were sent back, my heart broke because I knew you'd be devastated. All I want is for you to find yourself Sarah, and stop worrying about what everyone else wants you to be. You enlisted to spite your father and I, but I knew it would happen eventually. You were a born leader. I hated seeing you shut yourself away during your recovery because you weren't you. You were a broken version of yourself."

"I still am. The doctors can't fix me," she argued.

"You're right." Olivia said, nodding, "They can't fix you, because you have to fix yourself. You have to stop thinking you're not good enough."

"I don't know if that's possible."

Wiping tears off of Sarah's cheeks, Olivia smiled. "I bet if I ask those two brothers, they'd help me convince you."

Giggling she nodded, "Probably. They do seem to like me a bit."

"The older one, Silas, he seems a bit stiffer than Jeremy," Olivia said. "Was that because of me?"

"No, it was because of me. That was the first time I'd been put in a situation where I needed to classify our relationship. We haven't been seeing each other long."

"And how exactly would you classify your relationship?" her mother asked, lifting one eyebrow.

"I'm head over heels in love with them, Mom, but I haven't told them everything yet." She hiccupped through her tears, "They don't know that I have more surgeries ahead of me. What if they don't want to deal with all of that?"

"Then they're not the men for you," Olivia said firmly. "You know, when I met your father I was a young girl just out of high school with dreams of marriage, kids, and a white picket fence. I had no idea how to be a Navy wife. When Brian asked me to marry him, I turned him down. For almost three months I pushed him away."

"Why?"

"Because I was scared of failing him. I'd never even been away from home. Being a Navy wife meant being on my own a lot while he was on assignment, and it meant moving from place to place with no choice in the matter and no way to plant roots for stability. It scared the hell out of me."

Accepting a tissue from her mother's purse, she sniffed. "How did he convince you?"

"He offered to leave the Navy."

Sarah gasped in surprise. "But he loved being in the Navy."

"Yes, but he loved me more. That's when I knew that there was no way I could let him slip away. Loving means being willing to sacrifice. I loved him enough to sacrifice my dreams of a white picket fence." Her mom paused, and hugged her again. "You have to let them decide if they love you enough. And besides, the doctors only warned you that there's a chance you might need more surgeries in the future. They never said it was for sure."

"I love you, Mom," she whispered into her mother's neck.

"I love you too, honey. Now, I need to call your father and have him make the drive down here. I think he needs to meet your beaus in person. Maybe we can all have dinner tomorrow evening?" Olivia suggested, pulling her cell phone from her purse.

"I think that would be great. Do you mind if I go make peace with a couple of fantastic guys whose feelings I might have hurt this evening? You're welcome to stay here tonight. You can take the bed and I'll take the sofa."

"I'll stay here on one condition," her mother said sternly. "You take the bed and I'll take the sofa—unless you end up sleeping over at someone else's house tonight."

Laughing, Sarah hurried to find her shoes and collect her own purse before she headed off to find her men. She had no idea what she was going to say to them, but sometimes winging it was for the best anyway.

CHAPTER NINE

SILAS HEARD SARAH'S CAR, but he stayed put. The gentle sway of the patio swing soothed his inner caveman who was hurt and pissed off, so he kept rocking away, ignoring the sound of the front door, and the murmur of voices inside. If she came to apologize she'd have a lot of groveling to do.

Walking in on her and Olivia was the most awkward moment of his life. It even superseded the time in junior high when he'd had to tell his mom he had jock itch and needed special powder to treat it. He'd felt like less than a man as she introduced him as a friend.

After the most beautiful two weeks of his life, she'd knocked the wind out of him in one precious moment. He'd been on the verge of declaring his own feelings for her when Jeremy did, but the fear in her eyes kept his tongue still. All this time, he'd thought they were all three on the same page, and he was devastated to realize they weren't.

He'd been trying to convince himself that her refusal to spend much time out on the town with them was just nerves, but now he wasn't so sure. Maybe she was ashamed of their unconventional relationship or maybe she just wasn't ready to admit they were actually in a relationship. It didn't matter. It hurt.

He heard the back screen door creak behind him, but he quietly sipped his beer, ignoring the patter of footsteps approaching. She hesitated next to the swing, and he got the sense that she was trying to figure out what to say to dig herself out of the hole she'd created.

"Silas?"

Flicking his eyes to her briefly, he noted her tearstained cheeks, and sorrow-filled eyes, but he didn't respond. He wasn't sure he could speak without breaking down.

"Silas, please talk to me. I know I messed up, but I didn't know she was coming to town, and she caught me off guard." Edging closer to him, she stopped directly in front of him, blocking the sunset from his view. Her silhouette made his cock twitch as usual, but his aching heart wasn't ready to admit it yet.

He knew she regretted what had happened. It was written all over her face, and the moment she dropped to her knees in front of him, and prettily whispered, "Please, Si, forgive me," his control broke, and he reached for her.

Drawing her between his knees, he held her by the back of her neck and kissed her passionately. His kiss was hard and demanding, and she accepted it, melting into him. When he finally released her, she slumped forward, bracing herself on his thighs.

"Sugar, I'm not angry. I'm hurt," he said finally.

Disappointment flashed on her face and she nodded. "I know. And I'm so sorry I hurt you."

He shook his head and huffed, "I'm not even sure you understand why I'm upset, sweetheart."

"I-I didn't explain to my mom who you and Jeremy were to me. I let her believe we were just friends." She paused, and then said, "But for the record, she knows the truth now."

He narrowed his eyes at her, and she wrinkled her nose.

"She was peeping through the curtains."

Fighting back a grin, he nodded. "Like mother like daughter. I'm glad you told her the truth. How did she feel about it?"

"She didn't seem fazed at all. In fact, she encouraged me to be happy." Sarah's eyes got a distinct shimmer in them, and she smiled. "You make me happy Silas, you and Jeremy."

Before Silas could continue the conversation, Jeremy stepped out of the shadows and joined them.

"You make us happy, baby, but you have to be okay with all of this in every way. Today, I told you I loved you and it scared you." His brother's face showed no emotion, but Silas knew he'd felt the rejection acutely.

"I'm sorry. I've never had anyone say that to me outside of my parents. It surprised me. I just reacted badly to everything." She sounded crushed, and it tore at Silas's heart.

Sarah Bryant was a strong woman, with an amazing sense of loyalty and pride. He loved that she had no filter, and that she was so responsive emotionally and physically. If he pushed her too hard, he'd break her, and he no desire to do that. It was a reminder that playing with the D/s lifestyle without her full understanding was only going to make a bigger mess of things.

Helping her to her feet, he kissed her forehead. "Why are you so scared to admit to the rest of the world that you're in a ménage relationship?"

"I'm not exactly..."

Jeremy let out a loud laugh. "Prove it, baby."

Silas shook his head. "We can't exactly make her wear a sandwich board around town."

"No, but we can take her out to dinner as a threesome. There will be no doubt in this town what that means to anyone that sees us," Jeremy said.

Considering his brother's words, Silas realized how smart the idea was. Sarah's fear was that she wasn't good enough for them, and that people wouldn't accept her as their woman. If they spoiled her and took her out all over town, she'd have to admit to herself that they wanted her for her.

Tipping her chin so that she had to look him in the eyes, he asked, "You're a soldier, so I know you've faced nightmares before. Why does this scare you so much?"

It was the question she'd been dreading, and yet it was the one at the root of the whole damn situation. She had to tell them the truth or she risked losing them both.

"I'm not good enough." She answered, refusing to meet either man's eyes. "I'm not a soldier anymore. I'm just Sarah Bryant. Part-time secretary, personal assistant, and disabled veteran."

"What the hell?" Jeremy said angrily. "Why would you say you're not good enough?"

"Didn't you hear the part about my disability? I'll never be able to function like before." She slapped at the scars adorning the lower part of her back, and tears pricked her eyes. "All because of one tiny piece of lead, I'm fucked for the rest of my life. I can't fulfill my dreams. I can't even get a decent job. I can't do what I wanted to do with my life."

Her body was trembling, and the tears were flowing down her cheeks now, but she'd opened up and it all seemed to be pouring out of her uncontrollably.

"You two deserve better. You'll want a family someday, and I can't guarantee I'll be able to carry a baby with my back problems. You both have good jobs that will support you into your later years. I have a job I got out of pity, and I'm ridiculously overqualified for it." She paused to take a deep breath, and started to move away from them, smacking Silas' hands away when he tried to hold her in place. "All my life, I wanted to be a soldier, and make a goddamn difference. And this"—she gestured toward her back where her scars were—"is what I get for it. Fucking sent home with a check that says, thanks but no thanks."

Her words cracked as she began sobbing, and fell back against Silas, his firm chest bracing her, and his strong arms holding her close. She heard him and Jeremy murmuring encouraging words to her, but she couldn't respond. The dam had broken, and there was no putting the water back now.

Every bit of resentment she'd held rushed through her. The anger and disappointment blazed into her chest, firing her blood before the icy cold reality of her situation put out the flames. She wasn't a soldier anymore. She was just a broken, sad woman.

At some point in her tearfest Silas lifted her and carried her inside. They secured her in bed under the blankets, bracketed by their large bodies. She didn't know how they'd feel about everything she'd revealed when the sun woke them in the morning, but she fell asleep to the sound of Silas's heartbeat in her ear and the feel of Jeremy's fingers stroking over her hip. Even though she'd fallen apart, they'd held strong and steady as always. Just letting her be.

CHAPTER TEN

Jᴇʀᴇᴍʏ ᴡᴏᴋᴇ up alone in bed with Sarah. He assumed Silas was fixing breakfast, but he wasn't curious enough to move from the cozy spot he was in. Kissing her naked shoulder, he considered everything she'd said before she fell asleep.

He was dumbfounded to realize that she didn't think herself good enough for them. He was just a tow truck driver, not a millionaire. Hell, he barely made forty thousand a year, and the only reason he had this big house was because he'd inherited it. It was more likely he wasn't good enough for her.

She shifted in her sleep, and sighed, the air rushing across his chest. The change in her breathing signaled her newly awake status, and he kissed her forehead.

"Morning, sunshine."

Tipping her head back, she looked at him warily. "Morning. Where's Si?"

"Cooking probably." He paused, but when she stayed quiet he added, "Are you feeling a little better after last night?"

"Um, does embarrassed count as better?" she asked with a snort.

"I don't get it. Why are you so hung up on being good enough? What's good enough?" he asked.

"I used to think I knew, but now..."

Silas entered the room carrying a tray that held a plate of biscuits, butter, jelly and coffee. "I figured we could talk while we ate breakfast. I didn't go crazy, but I know you need food in your stomach to take your medicine."

Sarah gave him a small, half-hearted smile as she sat up, and Jeremy saw Silas stiffen as he realized she'd withdrawn back into her shell this morning.

"Thanks. Coffee is good. I can't stay long. Mom's still at my place."

Exchanging a look with his brother, Jeremy shook his head. "If you're going, we're going with you, Sarah. It's time to face this head on. Today you introduce us to your mother—and not as old friends from your Army days."

"Okay," she said softly, catching them both off guard. She grinned over her coffee cup. "What? Did you think I was going to throw my coffee at you? Seriously, guys, I'm sorry about yesterday. I mucked it all up. If I'd known she was coming I might have handled it better."

"Would you have told her the truth?" Silas asked.

"I don't know. But it's a moot point now. Mom was going to invite my dad down to meet you guys, too. So, if my hysterical, girly moment last night scared you off, now is the time to give me the boot."

"Hysterical girly moment?"

"Give you the boot?"

Sarah laughed and shook her head, her dark hair bouncing on her shoulders. "I'm just giving you an out. I know I shared some stuff in the moment last night..."

"Like your fear that you can't have children?" Silas asked quietly.

She nodded, a guilty look crossing her face. "Yeah, like that. That's a doozy. The truth is they don't know if I'll be able to have kids or not. I don't really know if I want them, but it sucks to be told I might not be able to make that choice. I barely have the muscle strength to hold myself upright sometimes, so there's a chance my back won't take a pregnancy."

"That doesn't mean you can't have children, baby," Jeremy said.

"There are plenty of ways to have kids without actually being pregnant yourself."

Silas murmured his agreement and added, "Besides, we haven't even taken you out as a trio yet. I'm not sure any of us is ready to start talking baby names and nursery colors."

Her eyes grew wide, and she wrinkled her nose, "Sorry, I guess after Jeremy mentioned walking down the aisle yesterday I freaked. Everything happened at once, but that's no excuse for the freak-out. I've never cried so hard in my life. I don't know what came over me."

"It's actually pretty common for people suffering from PTSD to have emotional outbursts," Silas said, and Jeremy rolled his eyes.

"What he's trying to say, is that we're not bothered by the tears, baby. We're only bothered by the secrets. You have to talk to us."

"You guys keep saying that, but—"

"No buts," Silas interrupted. "Finish your breakfast and get dressed. Instead of making you orgasm today, we're going to make you play girlfriend all over town. By the time we're finished, there won't be a doubt that we've claimed you as our woman."

"Your woman? Like your property?" she said, narrowing her eyes.

"Not property," Jeremy corrected. "Gift. Privilege. Reward."

"All right, all right. Enough. I'll give it a try, but don't be surprised if you get strange looks. You two could do a lot better." She hurried into the bathroom leaving the two brothers to stare after her in frustration.

"She still doesn't get it," Jeremy said.

"Nope," Silas agreed. "But she will. We'll make sure of it."

No matter how many times the guys assured her that they were proud to be out with her in public, Sarah still felt awkward. She felt like everyone was staring at them as they tried to eat their lunch. Every time she lifted her head it seemed she caught someone else's eye, and even though most of them smiled pleasantly at her, she felt judged.

What kind of woman dated two men at once? And brothers no less?

It sounded twisted in her head, yet when she questioned which one she would give up if she had to, there was no doubt that she couldn't let go of her affection for either man. They'd somehow attached themselves to her soul in the last couple of weeks. The idea of not having them was almost scarier than facing a judgmental society.

"You're not eating." Silas noted, gesturing to her untouched plate of barbecue ribs and fries.

"It's hard to concentrate on eating when people are staring at us," she hissed, not even trying to hide her annoyance. "It might not bother you, but it's driving me crazy."

"Who is staring, baby?" Jeremy asked, turning almost one hundred and eighty degrees to peer at the other patrons in the diner.

"Stop it! It will only make things worse if I point them out."

"I think you're paranoid." Silas said simply. "If anyone is staring this way it's because you look absolutely beautiful in that dress."

"Do you know how long it's been since I wore a dress?" She fidgeted with the low neckline of the sundress, wishing she hadn't gained those extra twenty pounds since her injuries.

"You should do it more often." Jeremy said, giving her a brilliant smile. "Makes me hard just knowing I could lift your dress and slide right into your hot pussy."

Sarah glared back at him. "Only insane people dislike underwear."

"Then call for the straight jacket, baby, because I definitely dislike underwear on you." He said, winking her way.

Their morning conversation had become a battle of Dominance, which the guys had ultimately won. She'd had no intention of following through with their instructions to go pantyless under a dress, but when she came out of her bedroom dressed, Silas had done a spot check on her. She was just thankful that her mother was at the Mercantile getting a few extra supplies she'd need for her extended trip, because that discussion would have been a nightmare.

"Eat your lunch, Sarah," Silas said firmly.

Stabbing a fry with her fork, she stuffed it into her mouth just as another woman caught her eye from across the room. The disapproving frown on the other woman's face set Sarah off, and she dropped her fork with a loud clink.

"I'm done eating. Can we leave please?" she grumbled.

Jeremy and Silas exchanged confused looks before Jeremy asked, "What just happened?"

"Nothing. I'm just not hungry."

Silas shook his head. "You were irritated before, but now you're furious. Talk to us Sarah."

"That woman over there, the one with the permed hair, she keeps looking this way and frowning. I don't like being scrutinized by someone I don't know."

Discreetly glancing over, Jeremy's face turned a bright shade of red. "Holy shit. Si, that's Minnie."

"Who's Minnie?" Sarah asked, but Silas was already standing and walking toward the woman with his arms spread wide.

"Our aunt, come on, I'll introduce you." Before she could protest, Jeremy was dragging her from the table across the diner to Minnie's table. He released her long enough to embrace the small woman in his arms. "Hey Minnie! Good to see you."

"Hi boys. I'm good, and Walt is meeting me here shortly for lunch. He had an appointment with Dalton this morning." Minnie held her hand out to Sarah with a polite smile. "Hello dear, I'm Minnie White, and I'm sorry I interrupted your date."

"Nice to meet you Mrs. White." Sarah said, ignoring the second half of her statement. "I'm Sarah Bryant."

"Are these boys taking good care of you?" Minnie asked, giving both men a pointed look. "Because if they aren't, they'll have to answer to me and their Uncle Walt."

"Of course we're taking care of her," Silas protested. "Isn't that right, sugar?"

"As well as can be expected. They're certainly gentlemen when we're in public," Sarah said, just barely resisting rolling her eyes.

Minnie laughed. "Well isn't that what all ladies want? A man who is a gentlemen in public and a badass in the bedroom."

Sarah felt her mouth drop open in shock at hearing that particular statement come from the older woman, and beside her, Jeremy and Silas both laughed.

"Oh shoot. I've gone and embarrassed you now," Minnie said. "Don't mind me, Sarah. I'm just a doddering old woman with foot-in-mouth disease. Walt swears the connections between my brain and mouth are backwards. I'm constantly speaking before I think."

"No ma'am. I'm not embarrassed exactly—"

"Ma'am? Oh, no! Heavens, please call me Minnie. Ma'am makes me feel ancient."

"Minnie then, you just caught me off guard," Sarah explained.

"I do that sometimes. I figure it's good to keep people on their toes so that they don't start thinking of me as predictable," Minnie said with a wink. The gesture was so similar to one Sarah had seen Jeremy make that she smiled in response.

"Hey Minnie, if you and Walt don't have any plans for the evening, why don't you come over to our place?" Silas offered. "Sarah's parents are in town, and we're going to host dinner. We'd love to have you join us." Sarah's mouth dropped open once again.

"That would be wonderful!" Minnie exclaimed with a loud clap. "It's been ages since we caught up. Are you sure you don't mind the extra people? I mean, if this is a private dinner..." She looked at Sarah for approval, clearly understanding that Silas had thrown her a curveball.

"No, no, that would be great. Um, I'd love to meet Walt, too. I didn't realize the guys had family here in Stone River," Sarah said, fumbling to cover her unsettled emotions. It was bad enough she was going to introduce the guys to her father, but to have the awkward moment happen in front of strangers was significantly worse.

"Just Walt and I. What time should we be there?"

Silas glanced at Sarah but she could only shrug. "Let's say seven. I'll call you if that won't work. Your dad will be in town by then, right sugar?"

She nodded. "Mom said he should be here by four."

"Can I bring anything?" Minnie asked. "Pecan pie perhaps?"

"Oh you don't need to—"

"That would be awesome!" Jeremy interrupted Silas before he could stop Minnie's kind gesture. He grinned at Sarah and wrapped his arm around her shoulders, pulling her in for a side hug. "Minnie's pecan pie is the best in the world."

"I can't wait." Sarah said, hoping she sounded enthusiastic. Inside, she was feeling rattled. When the guys had talked about her going out with them as their girlfriend she hadn't really expected it to mean being introduced to family. Now they were having a joint dinner party and she hadn't even told her father she was dating two men yet. Holy hell, this was FUBAR.

Lost in her own thoughts, she didn't even notice when the conversation wound down, and the guys told Minnie goodbye. She managed to smile at the other woman before they hustled her back to their table. In spectacular fashion, they'd managed to overwhelm her with new things, and now she didn't know how to respond to all of it. Loving them was easier when no one else knew about it. How was she supposed to keep things the same if they kept changing them?

Silas was seriously concerned about Sarah's emotional state. Ever since lunch she'd been unusually quiet, even when they'd taken her for ice cream at Dottie's, and then for a walk through the town's one and only park. Each time they encountered someone new, she seemed to clam up even more, and he was afraid they'd pushed the limits with the dinner plans.

It was too late to change them, but it was never too late for a distraction. So as soon as they made it back to their place, he took Jeremy aside for a quick planning meeting.

"She's backtracking."

Jeremy nodded. "Yep. Meeting Minnie seemed to scare her."

"I'm not sure if it was that, or being forced out of her comfort zone all day long," Silas said, frowning in Sarah's direction. She was sitting on the back swing in her pretty sundress; the afternoon sunshine highlighted her dark hair and pale skin. Her bare foot lazily pushed the swing, and he couldn't help his deeply emotional reaction to the image. "We have to fix it fast, or tonight is going to be a clusterfuck."

"Her dad should be in town shortly. I'm not sure we have time." Jeremy watched Sarah with the same intensity that Silas felt, and his usually jovial spirit seemed sad. "Si, I'm not sure she's ever going to be the submissive we want."

The air rushed from Silas's lungs like he'd been gut-punched. "What are you saying?"

"I don't know. I'm head over heels in love with the girl, but damn it, I always planned on marrying someone who shared my kinks. If she hates being with us, how are we going to make this work?"

"She enjoyed what we did. You and I both know she's a submissive," Silas argued.

"Yes, but she's not ready to admit it yet, which means we're going to be in a constant state of turmoil until she is. On top of that, she doesn't even want anyone to know we're seeing each other. It's like she's ashamed of being with the two of us." Jeremy's body language was broken, and suddenly Silas felt the impact of his brother's words.

"I can't let her go."

"You can't make her stay."

Growling in frustration, Silas rubbed his hand over his scalp, trying desperately to come up with a solution. "Maybe we just need to back off a bit. Give her more time with each of us alone to grow more comfortable with the idea?"

"How do you plan to do that? We've only got a couple hours until our house will be full of family. They're not going to be very supportive if we're all looking like heartbroken teenagers."

"I've got a plan, but I need you to trust me." Silas said, "It's going to mean you making yourself scarce for a little bit."

Jeremy started to shake his head, "I don't know. Your plan earlier ended up getting waylaid..."

"Give me an hour. Then I'll back off and give you time with her. If we can't work through this, we'll lay it all out for her and let her make the call. I'd rather have a broken heart than force her into a life she hates," Silas said firmly. Jeremy nodded in agreement, and headed off into the house leaving Silas alone with Sarah.

Taking a deep breath, he focused on tempering his Dominant side, and drawing on the lover she needed right now.

She looked up when he took a seat next to her and drew her against his side. "Hey Sarge. Where's Jeremy?"

"He had a few things to do, so he's letting me sneak in some quality time with you. Is that okay?"

Nodding, she gave him a half-hearted smile. "Sorry, I guess I'm not very good company right now."

Resisting the urge to comment, he just gave the swing a firm push, and nudged her head into the crook of his shoulder. Snuggled together on that swing, he could almost forget every worry he'd had moments ago. In his mind's eye he could see decades of evenings spent on the swing, talking, laughing, and crying with Sarah. How could he make her see that, too?

"I love you," he murmured.

"I know."

"That's not usually the expected response."

"I..."—she paused—"I have deep feelings for both of you. I want you both in my life. I'm just scared of exactly what that means."

"Are you talking about the ménage aspect, or the BDSM aspect?"

"Yes, and just being in a relationship. I don't even love myself right now," she said wistfully.

"First of all, we've got to get you over your self-confidence issues. You're perfect for us, but you have to accept that you're worth loving. Second, the BDSM isn't necessary to our relationship. I hope you know that. Is it something Jeremy and I have both found that we enjoy? Yes, but if it means losing you, we'd give it up in a heartbeat."

"And how do I ask you to do that? You know I enjoyed what we did earlier, but I'm not sure I want that all the time."

Silas considered her words. He'd assumed a lot when he'd pushed her into submitting earlier. While she had agreed to play the submissive role, he hadn't really taken time to teach her what it meant, or why he wanted it from her.

"You're right. I think we need to step back and consider what's best for all three of us. If you'll consider going to The Cage for an evening, I can work out a few sessions with various long-time couples. They can help all of us understand how to make things work. Parker and Rachel go there a lot, and Tanner and Zoey are members, too. I'm pretty sure Ryker and Mack have been, but I don't know if they've taken Claudia yet. Ménage is only one aspect of what we're asking out of this relationship, but it's the most important part. If you can't be comfortable with both of us as your boyfriends—"

"Stop. I've been thinking about that all day long. I'm not going to lie and say I'm completely okay with it yet, because I want to be honest here, but I can't see myself picking one of you over the other. I lo–care for both of you so much. I guess I'm scared of what other people will say when they see us together. All day long I kept looking for people watching us or smirking at us."

"In Stone River you're unlikely to see much of that."

"But what about in the rest of the world? Surely you don't plan to spend every minute of the rest of your life in Stone River?" she protested. "How do we book a vacation for three, when packages are sold to couples? Who has sit in the back seat when we go somewhere?"

Silas frowned at her in confusion. "Jeremy and I both drive trucks—"

"But I have a car, with two front seats. Who am I supposed to let sit next to me, and who has to take the back?"

"Sarah, you're seriously overanalyzing this," he said with a laugh. "We'll take everything and every situation one day at a time, but if you're always second-guessing, you'll never be able to completely embrace it."

"And what happens then?"

"I won't answer that, because I don't think we'll have to face that. I think you've hidden yourself away in your shell for so long that you're scared to come out now. Hiding doesn't make the issues go away, you know?"

She nodded. "Boy, do I know that. If that were the case, I'd be back in the sand on patrol by now."

"So that's what you'd want if not for your injuries? To go back overseas?"

"Wouldn't you?"

Silas shook his head, "No. Now that I've found you, I can honestly say I wouldn't want to be separated from you for that long."

Sarah's mouth dropped open, and she stared up at him in surprise. "Seriously?"

"Dead serious."

"Whoa. That's a big statement Sergeant White. You were a hell of an Army medic. I was surprised you'd given it up at all."

"I realized that fighting didn't make me happy. It was helping people that satisfied my soul. I can do that back here on American soil." He paused, and dropped a kiss on her full lips. "What makes you happy, Sarah?"

Her eyelids dropped heavily, and she sighed against his lips. "You. You and Jeremy make me happy."

It was exactly what he was hoping to hear, and he grinned down at her, pleasure filling his chest. "Let me make you happy, Sarah." Lifting her onto his lap, he gripped her chin and held her in place for a deep kiss.

Her hands came up to grip his shoulders for balance, and she relaxed into the kiss, opening for him and tangling her tongue with his. He loved the way she felt in his arms, and his body responded.

Tugging at her hips to draw her closer, he felt her spread her knees, and he groaned when her hot cunt settled over the zipper of his jeans. The reminder that she was completely bare beneath her dress made him horny as hell, and he released her face to slide his hands under the hem. Holding her ass in his hands, he pushed the swing with his foot, and they rocked together, the motion of the swing making them thrust against each other until they were both panting.

Without a word, he reached between them, and released his hard cock, taking a moment to stroke his finger up her wet slit, before he pulled her back against him. He dick slid between her spread labia, the head tapping her clit each time they moved. As much as he wanted to be inside her, he couldn't bring himself to push his way in without a condom on. That would be a violation of her trust, and they were already on precarious ground. Instead, he used the momentum of the swing and the pressure of his cock against her clit to stroke her. Alternating his hand placement from her sweet tits to her lush ass, he couldn't get enough of her, and when she finally exploded on top of him, soaking his jeans with her sweet cum, his body reacted instinctively. Sticky fluid shot up from between them, landing on the front of his t-shirt.

He groaned with his release, and let his head fall back to stare up into the sky. "Damn woman."

"Me? You started this, buck-o. Don't blame me for ruining your clothes," she said with a giggle as she climbed out of his lap.

"Where you going?" he protested, reaching for her.

"Oh, no you don't." She adjusted the top of her sundress so that her pretty tits were hidden again and shook her head. "It's bad enough the inside of my skirt is going to be wet for a while. I'm not snuggling up and ruining the dress. It's all I have to wear when company gets here."

"Guess we'll have to have you bring a few extra outfits over to leave here," he said with a wink, zipping his jeans and stretching his now relaxed body.

The back door opened, and Silas looked over to see Jeremy watching them with a wide smile. "Whatcha been doin' out here?"

"Bird watching." Sarah said, leaning down to kiss Silas one more time, before she turned and headed his way. Silas watched her hips sway with a newfound feeling of joy. This would work out. He just knew it.

CHAPTER ELEVEN

It took Sarah all of two minutes to realize that Jeremy was the cook in the White household. While Silas took the marinated steaks out to the grill, Jeremy moved flawlessly around the small kitchen whipping up various side dishes, and a divine looking chocolate pudding dessert. Swiping her fingertip through the whipped cream, she popped it in her mouth and hummed her pleasure.

"That's yummy," she told him, "Are you sure there's nothing I can do? I feel like a bum not giving you guys a hand."

Shaking his finger at her, Jeremy tucked the dessert in the fridge and then took her hands in his, kissing the finger she'd just been sucking on. "Thank you baby, but we have it handled. Tonight we just want you to kick back and relax. Get to know our family while we get to know yours."

He stared down at her with such emotion on his face that she felt her heart stutter in her chest. Running her finger over his full lips, she gave him a wink. "What if I want to tempt you out of the kitchen for a little bit? Do you have anything that might burn?"

Jeremy inhaled sharply and groaned, "Damn woman, you could tempt a saint. Hang on and I'll shut off the fire. We can sneak in a quickie if we hurry."

Sarah laughed as he moved like lightning, rushing around the kitchen to shut off the stove and the wall oven. She sent a silent prayer up to the heavens that dinner would still taste decent, and then let him lead her into the pantry.

They came together fast and hard, but she wasn't complaining. The sensation of the chest freezer under her ass was icy cold against her burning hot skin, but it gave her the perfect height for Jeremy to open his jeans, and run his cock through her damp folds. She arched her back, trying to force him inside of her, only to be waylaid when he pulled away.

"What are you doing?" she protested.

"Condom, baby. Just a second." His wallet hit the floor, contents scattering, but he held up the tiny plastic square triumphantly and ripped it open with his teeth.

Holding her skirt up, Sarah watched as he rolled the protection down over his hard shaft, and then eased it into her opening. They both sighed with raw pleasure when he filled her completely, and then their patience ran out. Fucking like bunnies on a freezer was a new high—or low—for her, depending on how she looked at it.

When he reached down between them to tease her clit, she had to bite her lip to keep from climaxing too fast.

"Let go, Sarah, let me hear you. I want to hear you say my name when you come for me," Jeremy growled into her ear. The smell of sex filled her senses, and the dirty words drove her closer to the edge. "Come on, baby. Come for me."

She exploded, clenching around him, her eyes snapping shut as her body arched backwards. Magic rippled through her just as surely as it had with Silas's gentle loving. She felt desired and cherished. Almost necessary.

Jeremy came a moment later, his large cock flexing inside of her passage with a strength that astonished her. There was nothing like the sensation of being packed full of a hard cock, and she was quickly beginning to crave it.

The sound of voices shattered their intimate moment, and Sarah's eyes widened when Jeremy blanched and pulled away.

"Shit. That's Minnie!"

Scrambling off the freezer, she hurried to right her clothes and reclip her hair to the top of her head in some semblance of order. "Are you sure? God I hope it's not my mom and dad already."

Jeremy winked down at her, and then kissed her hard. "Ashamed of me already and we haven't even tasted dinner yet."

"Ashamed of you? No, never. Terrified of my father? Definitely."

Accepting his hand, she followed him back into the kitchen. Relief washed over both of them when they found it empty, and Jeremy hurried to the sink to wash his hands before finishing dinner. Sarah headed toward the back door to greet their guests, hoping like hell they wouldn't smell the sex on her.

Beyond the sliding glass doors, Minnie stood with her arm around an older gentlemen, smiling up at Silas. Walt looked a lot like his nephews. In fact, she'd have probably pinpointed the relationship without being told they shared blood, but the familiarity did nothing to calm her nerves as she stepped outside.

"There she is," Silas said, holding out a hand to her. "Walt, this is Sarah Bryant, our girlfriend."

"Minnie told me you two boys finally found a woman to put up with you." Walt winked her way, and held his hand out. "Nice to meet you Sarah. Tell me, what's wrong with you?"

"Walt!" Minnie gasped.

"Aw, man!"

Sarah stared at him in confusion. "Sir?"

"Well, I figure there must be something wrong with you if you're interested in these two jackalopes. Pain in the ass to their poor mama all their lives." Humor sparkled in the older man's blue eyes, and Sarah laughed.

"I've got a few quirks and kinks to work out, but so far they suit me just fine." She warmed up to the couple quickly, finding it easy to exchange banter with Walt. Minnie stared at her husband with such affection and adoration that it touched her deeply. Did she look at the White brothers that way?

The sound of her father's booming voice made her jump, and she nearly landed on the grill she twisted around so quickly. If not for Silas's quick hands, she'd have had burn scars to add to her growing body art.

"Daddy!"

"Sarah-Bell!" Brian Bryant wasn't quite as large as the White brothers, but he had a strong bearing that was formidable to everyone he came across. His daughter, however, was the exception to that rule. She hurried over to hug him tight, inhaling his aftershave deep into her lungs.

"I'm glad you came," she said after he released her.

"Of course, baby girl. The way your mama tells it, you've got someone I need to meet." Brian looked up, his eyes narrowing on Silas behind her.

"Senior Chief Bryant." Silas held his hand out, "Silas White, and I see you've already met my brother Jeremy."

Jeremy was standing in the doorway looking just as awkward as the situation felt. Unsure what to say, Sarah scrambled to hug her mom. "Mom, this time, let me introduce the guys correctly. These are Jeremy and Silas White,"—she paused, and glanced at her father before she pulled herself straighter—"my boyfriends."

Olivia's face blossomed into a wide smile, and she nodded to her daughter before addressing the guys. "It's lovely to see you both again. Thank you for the invitation to dinner tonight. Brian and I were pleased to accept."

"Boyfriends?" Brian asked. "As in plural? You went and got yourself two of them?"

Swallowing her nerves, she nodded. "Yep."

For several breaths no one spoke. The steaks sizzled and popped on the grill as Brian and the two brothers faced off. Her father's eyes went back and forth from the men she'd fallen in love with to her, and she held her ground, patiently waiting for him to blow up.

"Not surprised it took two men to handle you."

Sarah stared at him in shock as everyone breathed a sigh of relief and laughed.

"Wait, what?"

Brian shrugged. "Stop fretting. Your mama filled me in on the way over here. Sarah-Bell, if these two fellas make you happy, then I'm happy." He narrowed his eyes on Jeremy and Silas, "But you tell me the moment that changes. I've got a dozen phone numbers of men who can make it look like an accident without blinking."

A giggle burst forth from her throat when Jeremy swallowed hard and fidgeted under Brian's hard look. "I don't know what to say." She threw herself into her father's arms hugging him tight.

"I love you, baby girl," he murmured, kissing her forehead before he turned to be introduced to Minnie and Walt.

Within minutes, the entire group was laughing and chatting like they were old friends. Sarah stood back watching, feeling freer than ever before. When had she suddenly found herself again? Was it because of Jeremy and Silas, or was she finally accepting the life she'd been given? It all seemed so perfect, yet a tiny niggling doubt still held its place in her brain. How long would this last?

"So Minnie, do you and Walt have children?" Olivia asked as they all sat down at the table to eat.

The sudden change in mood was so drastic that Sarah felt tears burn her eyes. Clearly Olivia had misstepped with her question.

Minnie's eyes grew shiny, and Walt reached for her hand, answering for her. "We had a son. Benjamin, but he passed as a young boy."

"I'm so sorry." Olivia said, covering Minnie's other hand with her own. "Was it an illness?"

Walt cleared his throat before explaining. "No, it was actually an accident. He'd gone swimming down at Devil's Drop—it's a local swimming hole—anyway, he lost his footing and fell. Hit his head on the way in, and that was it."

"Wow. I can't even imagine what that was like for you both," Olivia said, reaching out to her husband with her other hand. "I remember that morning when we got the call about Sarah's injury. The fear that went through me was bone-chilling. I was just sure they were going to call back before we could get on the plane to Germany and tell us we'd lost her."

"I didn't realize you had been injured, Sarah," Minnie said, dabbing her eyes with a napkin, clearly glad for the change in subject.

Sarah felt her nose wrinkle up in distaste of the new topic, so she looked down at her plate. "Yeah, it wasn't that big of deal, just one little bullet."

"One little bullet that did a hell of a lot of damage," her father interjected. "Several surgeries to repair everything from a broken spine to a shredded kidney and all sorts of internal dings that had to be fixed. Damn near lost her on the table twice, but the Army has damn good surgeons. That's about all they've got going for them."

"Dad," Sarah warned.

"Well, they are still the Army. Now, if you'd have been on a Navy vessel when it happened—"

Olivia slapped Brian's hand, "Enough of that. We're not getting into that argument here."

"Thank you," Sarah said, glaring at her father. "As for my injuries, they were far better than they could have been. At least I came home on two feet."

"Amen," Silas said, smiling her way.

"I'll drink to that." Jeremy tipped his soda her direction and winked at her.

"You must have had a guardian angel with you that day, Sarah. For you surely are blessed. I know several families who've lost loved ones overseas," Minnie said. "Did you stay in the military after that?"

"No, actually, they gave me the boot. I came down to Stone River because I was hoping to find work based on an ad I saw. Thankfully, that job didn't work out, and Claudia Thompson hired me as her assistant," Sarah explained.

"Oh that's lovely!" Minnie said with a clap, "I adore the Thompson family, their new baby Denver is darling."

"They've been good to me, and I enjoy the work. I wish it was more physically demanding, but..." she shrugged.

"Your doctors said you should take it easy rebuilding you physical capabilities," Olivia said sternly, "You're not pushing yourself too hard are you?"

"Of course not, Mrs. Bryant," Silas jumped to her defense, "Jeremy and I are seeing to it that she rests. Actually she and Jeremy are planning on working out together so that he can help monitor her progress."

Sarah gaped at him. "Not exactly—"

"Sure, yeah, I'll even tag along to the next doctor's appointment and clear it with him to make sure she's in fighting shape. You've got nothing to worry about with her in our care." Jeremy continued as though she wasn't even there, and her temper flared.

"What the hell?"

All eyes turned her way, the looks a mishmash of confusion, and amusement.

"Since when do I need a keeper? I'm not broken damn it," she snapped.

Silas's eyes gleamed. "Right you are. And I'll remind you of that every time you try to tell me you are."

Instantly, she realized that she'd backed herself into a corner. For the last couple of weeks she'd pushed them away based on the fact that she felt like she wasn't whole enough for them, and she'd just proclaimed herself in fine shape. If she wasn't broken, then what was she?

"Excuse me, I need a –um, just, yeah..." Pushing away from the table she hurried out of the dining room and straight out the back door, walking away from the house without a destination in mind. She just needed more space to breathe.

"Sarah!" Jeremy called out. She could hear the two men gaining on her, but she was at a loss as to what to say to them right now, so she didn't stop. When Jeremy grabbed her hand and spun her around, she gasped.

"What!"

He frowned at her, looking slightly hurt at her attitude. "What are you running from, baby?"

"You. Your brother."

"Do we scare you?" Jeremy asked as Silas joined them. The two men boxed her between them, holding her in place with just their presence, but neither touched her.

"No! Damn it. I scare myself. You guys make me want things, and you make me think that I deserve them."

Silas shrugged. "What's wrong with that?"

"I—I—"

"I'm only going to say this once, Sarah Bryant, so you'd better listen. There is nothing wrong with you. The injuries you survived make you stronger, not weaker. The scars make you more beautiful, not ugly. I want who you are now, not the woman you wanted to become when you joined the Army." Jeremy's words caught her off guard. Not just what he said, but the way he said it. He meant it.

"You didn't know me before. I could have been an officer," she protested.

"But then you wouldn't have come back home, or come to Stone River, and I wouldn't have you here with me now." Looking up at his brother, Jeremy continued, "Silas and I want you, but we don't want the chip on your shoulder."

Tearing her eyes away from him, she focused on a spot in the distance as her thoughts spun in her head. Could she really accept that they saw her as more than she could see herself? For two years she'd focused on how broken she was, and now they wanted her to accept how strong she was.

"Please let it go, Sarah. Let us love you for you." Silas murmured, wrapping his arms around her and pulling her back against his chest. He kissed her temple and whispered, "Love me. Love us. Please."

"I do," she heard herself answer. "More than I can even say. If you can accept me as I am, then how could I not?"

Jeremy's face burst into a grin, and he tore her from Silas' arms, spinning her around in the air. "Goddamn woman, you sure know how to make a guy sweat!"

Laughing through a thin veil of tears, she kissed him. "What happens now?"

Silas, turned her so that he could tip her chin, and kiss her gently.

"Now we go back inside and tell your mother and my aunt that they get to help us plan a wedding."

"Sergeant White, are you asking me to marry you?"

"Damn straight. Are you saying yes?" he asked, staring into her eyes without blinking.

She nodded. "Abso-freaking-lutely."

The End

Crawley Creek Series

Beginnings

Forget Me Knot

Rough Ride Romeo

Claiming His Cowgirl

Sunnyside Up

Hawke's Salvation

Handcuffed by Destiny

Fetish & Fantasy

Watching Sin

Submission Dance

Mistress Hedonism

Masquerade

Surrender Series

Weekend Surrender

Flawless Surrender

Primal Surrender

Broken Surrender

Fantasy Surrender

The Gray Pack Series

Fire of the Wolf

Reflections of the Wolf

Legacy of the Wolf

Dreams of the Wolf

Caress of the Wolf

Honor of the Wolf

Apache Crossing

Sidney's Triple Shot

Sunset Point

Point of Seduction

Tempting Tanner

www.LoriKingBooks.com

SIGN UP FOR LORI'S FREE NEWSLETTER!

ABOUT THE AUTHOR

Best-selling author, Lori King, is also a full-time wife and mother of three boys. Although she rarely has time to just enjoy feminine pursuits; at heart she is a hopeless romantic. She spends her days dreaming up Alpha men, and her nights telling their stories. An admitted TV and book junkie, she can be found relaxing with a steamy story, or binging in an entire season of some show online. She gives her parents all the credit for her unique sense of humor and acceptance of all forms of love. There are no two loves alike, but you can love more than one with your whole heart.

With the motto: Live, Laugh, and Love like today is your only chance, she will continue to write as long as you continue to read. Thank you for taking the time to indulge in a good Happily Ever After with her.

SIGN UP FOR LORI'S FREE NEWSLETTER!

Find out more about her current projects
lorikingbooks.com

RED HOT HEROES
COLLECTION

www.RedHotAuthors.com

BROKEN SURRENDER by LORI KING

One bullet made it physically impossible for Sarah Bryant to fulfill her dreams of a military career. With her family's sympathy suffocating her, she escapes to Stone River, Texas, determined to rebuild a life and maybe find a new dream.

Silas and Jeremy are two brothers who are as different as Texas is big. One is an adrenaline fueled former Army medic, the other is a laid back tow truck business owner. The two things they have in common? They know they want to live life in a ménage relationship, and Sarah is the woman for them.

Sarah has too many doubts about herself to believe she can be enough for one man let alone two. Can these souls find what they need to grow together, or will they leave more emotional scars to match their physical ones?

www.LoriKingBooks.com

STARTING OVER by MAGEN MCMINIMY

After running from the one man who could have mended her heart, Callie Sullivan has been finding comfort in her best friend, D. When heartbreaking news about D's deployed husband, Adam, makes its way to the states, Callie focuses on helping her friend learn to survive after tragedy strikes.

Recently returned from Iraq, Luke Merrick learns about the attack on his former sergeant and best friend, Adam. Knowing D will need all the support she can get, Merrick finds himself back where he lost the one woman he thought could be his future.

With D's heartache fresh and raw, now is hardly the time for Callie's past to resurface, bringing new danger to those whom she wishes to protect and help heal. But life rarely gives Callie what she needs.

This Veteran's Day, find home in the heart of our heroes with Starting Over part of the Red Hot Heroes multi-author series and stands alone for reading enjoyment.

www.MagenMcMinimy.com

PROMISE YOU by RENE FOLSOM

Danielle never realized just how much her brother meant to her until reality slapped her in the face, forcing her to wake up and pay attention.

After a shattering tour overseas, Dylan returned home to live with Danielle. Knowing he needed more care than his sister could provide, Dylan invites his battle buddy, Travis, to come live with them.

After a rather unorthodox meeting, sparks begin to fly between Danielle and Travis. However, both of them know just how difficult it will be for their relationship to blossom without Dylan's blessing, leaving them conflicted about how far they want to take it. Travis wants nothing more than to earn Dylan's approval—to promise that he will cherish her —always.

Once Travis realizes he can no longer keep his affection for Danielle a secret, things become complicated and the boundaries between friendship and love cloud his future.

This Veteran's Day, find home in the heart of our heroes with *Promise You*, part of the Red Hot Heroes multi-author series and stands alone for reading enjoyment.

www.ReneFolsom.com

Report For Booty by Jodi Redford

Mason Gamble and Nash Vincent are pros at making people sweat. As former Army Rangers who run the toughest, ball-busting fitness boot camp in Michigan, they take great pride in that fact. But thanks to the knockout brunette housesitting next door, suddenly they're the ones experiencing excess perspiration. Fortunately, the perfect opportunity to be neighborly presents itself courtesy of a package delivery snafu.

Regan Wallace has trust issues. Specifically, trusting that her best friend *won't* make good on her threat to send a Strip-O-Gram for Regan's birthday. Is it any wonder she'd jump to the wrong conclusion when two gorgeous, camo-garbed hunks land on her front doorstep? Woops. The crazy part? They don't seem the least bit scandalized or offended by her boneheaded blunder. Judging by the sinful heat in their eyes, they're all too happy to provide her with a little two-on-one dirty dancing. For a woman recovering from a bad breakup, fielding the interest of two sex-on-a-stick men is both surreal and exhilarating. Indulging a three-way fling? Completely out of her comfort zone. But with her stay limited to a week, some no-strings-attached sex might be precisely what she needs to get her confidence back in stride.

None of them are prepared for the consequences of a sexy fling feeling like so much more. As Regan's stay draws closer to an end, Mason and Nash realize there's no way in hell they're letting the perfect woman slip through their fingers. And when it comes to fighting for her love, there are no fitter warriors for the ultimate battle to her heart.

http://www.jodiredford.com/More_Books.html

SNAKE'S SALVATION by Aliyah Burke
Two people with painful pasts can create something spectacular with each other.

Jason "Snake" LaRue was a Navy SEAL. Now he's not and he has trust issues and memories he can't forget no matter how hard he tries. His one solace is a woman who works at the local diner who chases away the darkness in him. But would she ever consider a man with his past?

Loretta Swann has given up art and now works at an all-night diner. Running from her past, she up and goes when the mood strikes. Her one shining moment a day is when the ex-SEAL graces the establishment. An impulsive kiss makes her wonder about something more with him. But when she learns what he wants, will she run again, or stick around to be Snake's Salvation?

www.aliyah-burke.com

HER HERO by Miranda Marks

Nate Morrissey has seen all kinds of action in his years with Marine Special Operations, yet nothing compares to the adventure he has at home with his new wife—what little time he's been home in their brief one year marriage. When he gets called out on a new mission at the beginning of a long awaited leave, his bride lays down an ultimatum. Unfortunately for them both, duty wins.

Becca soon realizes she wasn't meant to be a military wife. She thought she was strong, but the long months praying and waiting for his safe return have left her broken. When he leaves her yet again, she knows it's time to call it quits, no matter how much her heart tells her to stay.

Nate isn't ready to let go of his wife just yet. The fire they share is too hot to ignore. Nate comes home to an empty bed, but refuses to let it stay that way long. Till death do us part means something to Nate and he's not dead yet...

www.authormirandamarks.com

---

www.RedHotAuthors.com

Printed in Great Britain
by Amazon

83743056R10081